Blair J Collins was born and raised in Essex, living near the Thames Estuary. This is the sequel to his first novel, *A Coastal Shelf*. Following a long career in the fire service, he retired to focus on his writing.

Blair and his partner divide their time between the UK and Germany.

To all the marginalised, who have to fight their corner

Blair J Collins

GETTING AWAY WITH IT

AUSTIN MACAULEY PUBLISHERS

LONDON * CAMBRIDGE * NEW YORK * SHARJAH

Copyright © Blair J Collins 2025

The right of Blair J Collins to be identified as author of this work has been asserted by the author in accordance with sections 77 and 78 of the Copyright, Designs and Patents Act 1988.

All rights reserved. No part of this publication may be reproduced, stored in a retrieval system, or transmitted in any form or by any means, electronic, mechanical, photocopying, recording, or otherwise, without the prior permission of the publishers.

Any person who commits any unauthorised act in relation to this publication may be liable to criminal prosecution and civil claims for damages.

This is a work of fiction. Names, characters, businesses, places, events, locales, and incidents are either the products of the author's imagination or used in a fictitious manner. Any resemblance to actual persons, living or dead, or actual events is purely coincidental.

A CIP catalogue record for this title is available from the British Library.

ISBN 9781037106972 (Paperback)
ISBN 9781037106989 (ePub e-book)

www.austinmacauley.com

First Published 2025
Austin Macauley Publishers Ltd®
1 Canada Square
Canary Wharf
London
E14 5AA

For all their insights, advice, and support in the creation of this novel.

In the UK: Sarah Chamberlain, Joanne Williams, Alison Loades and Joleen May

In Germany: Klaudia Seitz, Gaby Port, Sigi Sandmeir, Franz Brauchle and Bernd Sandmeir

1

"What do you lot want?"

It was the necessary aggression required when deterring anyone trying to gain entry to her safe haven.

The chain was on, her left hand fingered the edge of the door, and a cigarette glowed between her index and middle.

Luke reckoned seven stone wringing wet.

"We have been called, love, fire, smoke issuing. You alright?"

She removed her hand, remembering the pain when a door is quickly pulled, crushing the knuckles on the jamb, then shouldered inward, smashing it against your face. She left the chain in position.

"Ain't no fire. Clear off and leave me alone."

Linsey elbowed Luke out of the way.

"Hi ya, my name's Linsey. I'm the token woman who has to work with this bunch. If you drop the chain and open the door, I promise you I'll be the only one who steps inside."

The occupant had disappeared behind the door, but the cigarette smoke betrayed her position.

"We have to check. It's the job. Keeping you safe."

Linsey had removed her helmet and spoke directly to the elongated opening created by the door ajar. Her eyes looked up. She could discern an acrid tang emanating from within.

Perry appeared from the side alley.

"Can't see any problems around the back, Chris."

The officer in charge nodded.

"Keep me safe, eh, that's good of ya."

"Listen, if there's a fire in your house, I ain't leaving you in danger, but if there ain't."

"There ain't."

"I believe you. If there's no fire, we still need a look. I need to look. It will just be me, promise."

"If you're lying to me."

"Promise, just me."

The door moved closer to Linsey's face as the chain slid through the metal channel. Linsey looked at the rest of the crew. She was not in charge, but they knew she had command of the situation.

Chris Everett grabbed her arm.

"We don't know she's alone."

He placed his evacuation whistle in her hand.

"Blow that and we're coming in."

She nodded and stepped inside.

Three men stood by the front door; an emasculated group eager to reassert themselves should the Acme Thunderer let out a shrill warble of help. A wind blew a salad of dry leaves through their legs onto the hall carpet. Under the kitchen window, a skinny rose in a show of defiance refused to drop the last bloom of the year.

The autumnal equinox slipped by unnoticed.

"Send a message, Luke."

"Sure."

Luke turned towards the fire appliance and walked down the path. By the gate, he met a neighbour.

"Excuse me," he said, raising his hands that showed he came in peace.

"If it ain't you lot, it's the police," she said. "Trouble that one."

Luke nodded.

"Anyhow, it's me who called ya cos I see smoke coming out of her window." She pointed to the kitchen fanlight.

"You did the right thing, and we have it now so…"

She stepped aside.

An ice cream van stopped on the corner and let the annoying refrain of summer play through one more time.

Perry said, "The last two Sundays running, I've nodded off after my Sunday roast only to be woken up by one of those bastards." Chris nodded.

"What was you cooking?"

Linsey tried hard not to sound judgmental.

She was looking at the blackened frying pan in the sink. It was stuck to the yellow washing-up bowl. There was no sign of any food.

Seven stone wringing wet said, "Nuffin."

Ash from her cigarette, about to fall to the floor, was caught in her hand and laid in an ashtray; a leaf the colour of Caramac from the neighbour's beach hedge rolled past the kitchen door into the lounge.

"Turned the wrong ring on. Just wanted a cuppa."

"Alright, to open a window, give it a blow through."

The gesture, giving permission, was almost imperceptible.

Linsey stretched over the sink and opened the large window. She knew Chris outside would take it as a sign that all was well.

"So, you're alright, no burns?"

"It never caught fire, just stunk the place out, so you can go."

"Ok, long as you're ok. What's your name?"

"Christ, wot you the old bill now?"

"No, no, it's just the boss out there will need a name for his reports, you know."

Linsey thumbed over her shoulder.

"You can make one up if you like."

"You bloody make one up then."

Linsey looked at the kitchen table pushed up against the eggshell wall. It was accompanied by two chairs tucked neatly underneath each end. On the table, a mug containing a teabag sat next to a half-empty bag of white sugar twisted shut. The framed message on the wall above read, 'Love makes a house a home'.

A crack in the glass ran across the first word as though it had been struck out in a revised edit.

The two women stood looking at the message.

"Thanks," said Linsey.

"What for?"

"Trusting me. Anyway, I'm going now."

Linsey reached out a hand to touch the woman's shoulder, but she pulled back, so Linsey smiled and walked out the door.

Outside, Linsey was met by a smiling leading firefighter, Chris Everett. "Everything ok?" He asked.

She dropped the whistle in his hand.

"Yea, sweet," said Linsey as she walked away from the incident.

Perry edged the lorry passed the ice cream van, eyes peeled for any kids running out.

Chris Everett was letting control know they were available while Luke shouted at a young girl to stay on the pavement.

Linsey looked back at the house. Its front door and window shut tight once again. The net curtain in the kitchen looked discoloured, but not so the bedroom windows. They were bright white, the folds evenly spaced, and had been subject to the considered eye.

In the short time she had been in the fire service, one aspect of the job she liked most was how she stepped into people's lives. Not for long, and she hoped as far as the public was concerned, for positive reasons. One day, she would be standing in the grounds of a mansion because the daughter's pony had jumped in the pool, the next day in local authority accommodation helping the ambulance service get a bariatric patient down the stairs. The variety of work spiced her love of the job, but days like this were different. Today, she had stepped into a woman's life. A woman who was scared to open her door to authority or men; a woman whose fear or suspicion kept her stumm under the lightest interrogation.

The horse may be back in the stable, the fat man settled in his hospital bed, but the woman, her fellow sister, had been left as frightened and insecure as before they arrived.

Linsey felt a sense of failure as she stared out the window at nothing. "Couldn't even get her name."

"What!"

Her reverie broken, she turned and looked dumbly at Luke.

"I said what. What did you say?"

"Oh, I er...said I never got, I forgot to get her name."

"Patricia Arnold."

"How do you know?"

"Letter on the table by the front door. So, while you were inside doing your girlie chat, we were outside gathering info."

Linsey turned to gaze once again out to the street while pushing a two-fingered 'V' sign up the side of her face.

Luke smiled as he undid his tunic.

2

Eddie stood in front of the painting. The yellowed gold frame glowed bright against a grey-green flock wallpaper. A young Japanese girl nudged his shoulder, considered the artwork for twenty seconds, then moved on. An elderly gent stood directly in front of him, unapologetically obscuring his view. Eddie never moved.

A group of school children passed through the room, being ushered and shushed in equal measure by a staff of teachers whose idea of education had long been surrendered. Their sole intent now was to return to school with a full complement of kids.

It was over breakfast at his father's flat that he had read about the artwork, coming across the article about the nation's favourite painting while idly scanning the Tory rag for something worth reading.

"There ya go."

Ray placed a plate in front of him containing a fried egg, the edge of which resembled a brown lace doily, and budget baked beans that obscured two thin slices of white buttered bread.

"Thanks, Dad, looks delicious. Any more tea?"

"What your last servant die of?" Ray sat.

"Let me eat this before it gets cold, then I'll do you another."

With the table extended by two leaves, it was just big enough for the breakfast and necessary accoutrements. Eddie dropped the newspaper on the floor.

"What you reading?"

"Oh, nothing really, about a painting. Nation's favourite."

Eddie cut through the solid yoke and soaked it in the bean sauce. He had a slight hangover. What was left of the Irish whiskey he had brought with him the previous evening was safe in his father's kitchen cabinet. Its effects, diluted by a couple of pints of water before bed, had by and large been assuaged. The reason for their libation, as Ray put it, was the flat warming. A salutation to his new accommodation and new life. It was Eddie's first visit since he had helped his father move back to London.

"Cheers, Dad," he had said, raising the first glass.

"To…" he faltered.

"Home, Son, home."

Helping his father move had not proved the most arduous of tasks. Ray brought little with him from the family house in Stanford le Hope. His father had shed a skin, and Eddie had to admit he seemed younger for it.

The evening had started in a familiar way. Eddie had let himself in and, calling out, heard his father's familiar refrain.

"In 'ere, Son."

His father sat in a leather recliner, his feet on a matching stool, watching the news.

"Give me a minute."

Eddie threw his Barbour hold-all next to the new sofa and sat down. The living room of the ground-floor flat was a square box enhanced by what Eddie had to admit was cool furniture of his father's choosing from IKEA. Patio doors opened onto a personal paved area, then a communal garden. On the wall opposite the sofa and above the dining table was a photographic print of the *Prospect of Whitby*. It had been taken, Eddie guessed, mid-Thames at low tide. The wooden steps next to the famous pub leading to the stony foreshore were green with algae. A public house frequented by the likes of Pepys and Dickens.

Eddie wondered what they would make of today's London. Bigger, louder, and the churches familiar to them both were surrounded by canyons of glass and steel. The chroniclers of London's past stepping out of St Helen's Church Bishopsgate might not appreciate the science behind the oddly shaped buildings or the small transparent boxes containing people ascending and descending the sheer edifices, but would understand the wealth within and rightly guess at the poverty existing within the skyscrapers' lengthening shadows.

"Bloody Labour Party."

Ray broke Eddie's train of thought.

"What about it?"

"Tories in disguise."

"Yet, still you don't like 'em."

"Shouldn't pretend to be one thing when you're not."

Like happily married when you're not, Eddie thought, then decided to let it go. "Difficult being a socialist party in a capitalist society."

Ray looked at his son but wasn't interested enough to engage. Instead said:

"Look at this." Ray started to scroll. "All these channels. We have a communal ariel or whatever. Got hundreds."

He stopped at one showing *The Sweeney*. "Ah, don't make 'em like this anymore."

"Thank god," said Eddie.

"Believable characters, good plot, and no vomit."

"What?"

"Programs today must have someone vomiting and a scene in a toilet, a fight or something. It's compulsory. Can't make a drama without a toilet and vomiting."

Eddie joined in, adding to his father's plotline.

"So, man in a toilet talking espionage to another when a bloke comes in, throws up all over him, then a fight ensues."

"Only stopped when a woman enters because they do these days, go in the blokes, and shoots them all."

"Didn't see that coming, Dad."

"Tell ya, Son, write that and you'll have a hit on your hands."

The two men sat smiling, watching a Ford Granada racing through the dingy capital.

"Fancy fish and chips, Son? There's a nice one around the corner."

That was last night. Fish and chips, whiskey, and the TV.

Now with the plates collected, Ray called from the kitchen as he filled the kettle.

"What you doing today?"

Eddie was about to say he was at a loose end when he picked up the paper. "Well, seeing as I'm almost there, I think I'll pop into the National Gallery and see this great painting for myself."

3

"It's the right way up."

"Pardon."

"It's the right way up. Your head was leaning over to the right as though something was wrong."

"Oh, gotcha," said Eddie, before adding, "it's the nation's favourite."

"Evidently."

She was the same height as Eddie in her heels. Her black hair, centre parted, cupped her chin and extended over her collar, at the back. Her eyes were brown with the lightest of laughter lines fanning out towards her temples. Eddie was eager to take in her figure but knew how sleazy the top-to-toe scan looked, so he resumed his study of the painting.

"I know it's the right way up, obviously," he said. "But something ain't right and it's been bugging me since I saw a picture of it this morning in the paper."

"And what's that?" She held his gaze, having already given him the top-to-toe before engaging in this conversation.

"I've decided that can't be the sunset. Not from that viewpoint. That's the sunrise."

"It's allegorical. He knew what he was doing. The sun setting on the end of one era and the start of a new one. The steam ship is towing the sailing ship to its final berth to be broken up."

Eddie searched for a clever response.

"Lot of matchsticks."

Her full lips thinned as she smiled, the Cupid's bow collapsing into a smooth undulation.

"I don't think it was bought by Bryant and May, but I'll look into it."

"Do you work here?"

"Yes, and now if you'll excuse me, I have work to do. Enjoy the rest of your visit."

Before Eddie could think of another erudite remark, she was gone.

Eddie walked through the elegant rooms. He was conscious of the men and women staring at him across the centuries, demanding to be looked at.

'Who are you?' he would stop and ask. 'Would we be friends?' he wondered. He could read a name, but it meant little to him. The children were in front of a large painting of Henry the Eighth. Eddie knew him. Everyone did.

Outside again, he zipped up his bomber against the chill autumn air. He yawned and decided he needed some lunch.

He made his way through the throng of tourists, buskers, and pavement artists, mindful not to step on their masterpieces.

He started to walk the short distance to St Martin in the Fields, where in the beautiful crypt, he would queue for a sandwich made with bread his father would never contemplate. He waited for the lights to change at the start of Charing Cross Road. He could feel the thrum of the city in his chest. The buildings, once soot-covered, now blasted clean by high-pressure hose were revealed in all their majesty. His father's desire to return to the city of his birth, at first a surprise, was now obvious. Eddie felt it too. He imagined marine turtles covering thousands of nautical miles to return to the sand from where they once emerged. It's in us all, he thought.

He chose a pre-packaged beef sandwich with horseradish and rocket on rye and decided on a pot of tea.

He looked for a small deuce in a corner.

'Keep your back to the wall and your eyes on the door', his mother would say. She could have written that TV script in her sleep.

Annoyingly, all the gangsters had beaten him to his tables of choice.

He scanned the centre section in hope of an empty table and there, alone at a four, she was seated with her lunch and a book.

"Would you mind?"

She looked up.

"Oh, hi. Be my guest."

He sat diagonally across from her, thinking the angular dynamic would make it harder for anyone to join them. Eddie removed his lunch and placed his tray at the empty place in front of him. She continued to read, finding it difficult to finish the paragraph with this tall, dark stranger in her peripheral vision.

The hard noise from cutlery and china bounced around the room as the soft echoes of ghosts sighed in despair.

Eddie's teapot dripped onto the table as he poured. When he returned with a wad of serviettes, she had closed her book and was holding the coffee cup with both hands in front of her mouth.

"It's a great space, this. If I'm in the area, I like to pop down."

She took a sip and, placing the cup down, she said, "Well, that begs the question, do you come here often?"

"I thought that was the bloke's line."

"Not in this day and age. You're lucky I never preceded it with 'hallo darling'." Eddie took a bite. The phrase sounded incongruous on her lips.

"Well, do you?"

"No, if I'm honest, but now my father has moved back here, I might be more of a regular."

A man with a tray walked down their aisle and lingered by their table. His scrunched-up grey bucket hat and matching trench coat added to a guileless expression, but not his innate ability to read faces.

Eddie's face said, 'Don't even fucking think about it'.

The luckless fellow moved on; Eddie swallowed.

"Is this your regular haunt, lunchtimes?"

"No, too expensive for every day; most days, I don't get out at all."

"What do you do in the gallery?"

"Research."

"What, like, is this painting genuine?"

"Sometimes. Provenance is everything."

"Sounds interesting."

"Really? Most people would run a mile."

She placed her book back in her tote bag while asking, "What do you do?"

"I'm a painter."

"And decorator," she countered.

"Mainly marine scenes," was his counterpunch.

They looked at one another properly for the first time and smiled.

"I'm a firefighter."

"Oh, good pitch." She considered her coffee and decided against it before resuming her gaze.

"I am in Essex. What do you mean good pitch?"

He could see her considering her response.

"Boy meets girl, age is irrelevant, it's always boy meets girl. Let's say in a bar."

"Not a crypt."

"Not a crypt," she concurred.

"The boy engages her. You are chatting me up, right?"

"You asked me if I come here often."

"And I saw the look you just gave that guy."

Eddie felt himself blush. She continued.

"So, a witty opening line, 'can I buy you a drink', 'what's your name', then what do you do? The boy has to keep the humour and intrigue going, so I'm a fighter pilot or a brain surgeon. They laugh at the improbability; there might be a few more jokes, but the boy sadly has driven into a dead end. Fireman, however…"

"Fighter."

"Firefighter, it's plausible, interesting, and for most of us girls, sexy. So, good pitch."

Eddie finished his sandwich and took a swallow of tea. It was his turn to consider a response.

"I stood in front of that painting earlier, and while I admired it, that was where my appreciation stopped. Then, you engaged me and engaged me with the painting. Gave it meaning, context, and despite its age, relevance."

She nodded.

"Your explanation, or should I say your deconstruction, of what's happening here, though, well…"

"Cynical?"

"'Fraid so, and I do work in the fire service."

"Good for you."

She picked up her bag and made to go.

"Can I see you again?"

"Why on earth do you want that?"

"Because there is this painting I need explaining."

"Oh, which one?"

"It's called boy admires beautiful girl."

She stood.

"I know it. Though, never thought the girl was that beautiful, the boy though…"

"What? What about the boy?"

"Passable."

She reached into her bag and from her purse, gave Eddie her card.

Eddie read aloud, "Charlotte Barclay."

He looked up.

"Eddie Hart."

He stood and awkwardly put out his hand.

Charlotte took hold of his fingers. Eddie tried to softly enclose hers. The busy lunchtime noise faded, intensifying the silence between them.

Charlotte's face brightened into a tight-lipped smile and raised eyebrows.

"I got to." She nodded towards the exit.

Eddie reluctantly released his grip.

"I'll phone."

"It's my work number. You might get someone else."

She left, putting her coat on once she was clear of the table. She flicked her hair over her collar and was gone.

Eddie got out his new mobile phone. He dialled the number and after three rings, a woman answered.

"Research, Dorothea speaking."

"Is Charlotte there, please?"

"No, she is at her lunch. May I be of some help?"

"No, thank you. Just tell her Eddie Hart called."

4

It was the first day of the tour of duty. It consisted of two nine-hour days, followed by two fifteen-hour nights. Arthur Church was in the station officer's room, his room. It served as an office by day and a bedroom by night. It was 0830 hours. Arthur came in just after eight to let Len Duff, his counterpart on the Blue Watch, get away early. Before he left, Len informed Arthur that petty cash was required from the bank, and after carrying out the appliance inventories, they discovered the dust pan and brush were missing from the water tender. Apart from that, it had been a quiet night and everything was hunky dorly.

The correction never left Arthur's lips; he decided he preferred Len's version of the Welsh term.

Arthur sat back in the wheeled office chair, dropped his glasses from his forehead onto his nose, and started to scan the *FBU* magazine he had picked up from the desk in front of him.

There was a knock on the door before it opened.

"Morning, Guv."

It was Leading Firefighter John Mullins.

"Morning, John."

"Got a minute, Guv?"

"Sure, come in."

Eddie was walking across the yard from where he had parked his car. The rear bay doors of Langden Fire Station were open; he could see the three appliances housed and ready. They had been hosed and brushed clean, the bay floor was still wet from the mopping. Eddie chose to enter the station by the door that took him through the kitchen.

"Morning, Ken."

Ken was the mess manager on Red Watch, and it was his responsibility for their catering.

Ken was studying his accounts book. Without looking up, he exclaimed, "Cheeky git."

Eddie stopped.

"What, Ken?"

"Perry, cheeky git, never paid me last tour. Morning, Eddie. See that?"

Ken tapped the ledger.

"The importance of good bookkeeping."

"If I was you, I'd make him pay double this shift as a punishment."

Ken contemplated a sardonic reply, but a smiling Eddie was already on the way to his room.

In the watch room, the firefighters of Red and Blue waited for the end of one tour and the start of another come nine o'clock.

Eddie opened the door to his room as the door to Arthur's opened.

"Can you come in?" John Mullins asked.

Eddie slung his hold-all in his room before joining Arthur and John.

The three men exchanged pleasantries before Arthur explained why he requested Eddie's attendance.

John Mullins had been off work for the last two weeks, compassionate leave. His elderly mother, with whom he lived, had died. John was in his civilian clothes, which made Eddie assume he was asking for more time.

"John is slinging it in, Eddie."

Arthur looked at Eddie, keen to see the surprise on his face.

"Blimey, John, that's, that's terrible. You sure, John? I mean, if it's what you want, then great, but for us, that's terrible. Why? Sorry about mum by the way, but…"

John interrupted.

"I've had enough, Eddie, don't want to do it anymore. All the shitty things we see and do, all the aggro with the union. Sorry, Arthur, but you know I've never had the same love for it as you."

"Necessity more than love," replied Arthur.

"You know what I mean. Anyway, mum left that big old house to me and my brother, so we are selling up. With my half of the proceeds and my pension, I'll have enough to fuck off to Spain. So, yep, I'm slinging it in."

"When?" Eddie asked.

"Now. I gave a month's notice, and with the leave they owe me, that's it, I'm done."

Arthur Church stood.

"We are all going to miss you, John, especially today. You have been an excellent officer, a real asset to this watch, but I wish you all the best for the future."

"That goes for me, too," said Eddie.

"Thanks. Let's have a beer soon. No official leaving do, no memorabilia, I hate all that. Just the watch and maybe a few old friends from around the county."

John turned to leave, then stopped.

"Why are you going to miss me today, especially?"

"The dust pan and brush are missing from the water tender, I was going to ask you to order a new one."

It was more a guffaw than a laugh that accompanied a broad grin as he replied.

"Well, I can say it now. Go fuck yourself, Arthur."

Before Arthur could rejoinder, John Mullins stepped out the door and was gone.

5

"Can we come in?" Eddie called out.

The front door was ajar, and he could hear the cry of a young child.

In the living room, surrounded by his toys, was young Joshua. He was extremely upset despite his mother's attempts to calm him. It was that time in Joshua's life when his parents decided he needed to be potty-trained. In an effort to make this important step in his young life appeal to him, they had bought a potty that nestled in the seat of an appropriately sized plastic armchair. It was bright blue. Whether the toddler had removed the potty or not was unimportant. What was important was that Joshua had decided to stick his head through the hole in the seat. The blue plastic chair now sat squarely on his shoulders, his head where the potty should be.

It was the first shout of the day for the water tender, for which Eddie was in charge. Adam Martin was driving. In the rear of the cab sat Perry Jackson and Ken Taylor. They were arguing.

"I paid you."

"No, you didn't."

"I did."

"You didn't."

"I gave it to you first thing, like I always do."

"Then, why did I not enter it in the book like I always do?"

"Because you're a stupid old cunt."

Topography is an essential part of a firefighter's knowledge.

Having lived there all his life, Perry knew Langden like the back of his hand. "Second left, second right," he shouted to Adam.

Adam knew but always appreciated confirmation.

Eddie booked in attendance over the main scheme radio. Adam would stay with the lorry. Ken and Perry would accompany Eddie inside the house. Eddie lifted the gravity latch securing the garden gate.

"Anyway, Eddie says you got to pay double this shift."

Eddie stopped in his tracks.

"Will you two fucking shut up?"

When Joshua saw three huge creatures, all in black with shiny silver stripes reflecting the light from the TV, walk into his house, his alarm and his crying went up another level.

"Hallo, Mum," said Eddie.

"Hallo, mate," said Perry, kneeling next to Joshua.

"It's his potty seat, we can't get it off."

"Not training him very well," said Ken. His remark was drowned out by the crying infant and morning telly.

Eddie knelt opposite Perry.

Perry had been trying a few angles, but it was obvious the chair was not going to be lifted past Joshua's very red ears.

Perry looked at Eddie and, with the slightest shake of his head, conveyed this to him.

Eddie looked up at Ken.

"Go and get the small tool roll, please, Ken, and tell Adam to send an informative message to control. One small child with his head stuck in," Eddie hesitated.

"Khazi," suggested Ken.

"Toy, just say toy."

Joshua was tired; his cries, now a whimper, were all he had left.

"We are going to have to cut it off," Eddie told mum.

"That's ok," she said, stroking her son's sweaty head. "Couldn't get the little bugger to use it anyway."

As they were leaving, Eddie pulled Perry back.

"Did you pay?"

"Of course, I did."

"Can one of the others vouch for you?"

"Yea, of course."

Adam was sitting in the driver's seat. He lowered a window and called out, "Got a shout, chaps, car fire."

As they snaked across town, Eddie thought back to the last couple of days. His father, Ray, now ensconced in his retirement flat, had never appeared happier or content even after all those years locked into a marriage he never wanted.

There is a fire service message used at the end of large incidents. Such jobs may have lasted days, consisted of many crews and an inordinate amount of equipment. When all is done and the last appliance prepares to leave, the message is sent.

All gear stowed and duty left.

Eddie thought it applied to his old man. Following the tragic death of his mother last year, Ray had gradually put his affairs in order, sold most of the family possessions, and moved back to his beloved London.

All gear sold and duty left.

Did Eddie care? No, he had taken the few items that were important to him from the house and was glad his father was satisfying a long-held desire. What Eddie did care about was the wasted years when Ray was absent from his life; a father in name only, in sharp contrast to a loving, warm-hearted mother who doted on her only son. A bruising argument with his father earlier in the year had exorcised the pain in his heart and the misunderstanding in his head. To understand, to forgive, to move on. Both men were at the start of this journey.

They approached a roundabout. Eddie changed the two tones from the elongated wail to short whoops. He always did this when a change of direction was required. It was his audible signature.

Then, his chance meeting with Charlotte Barclay.

Thinking about her, and he did, a lot over the last forty-eight hours, released a little smack of adrenaline in the pit of his stomach.

It was exciting that she had started the conversation; she had noticed him. There it was again, the feeling.

Classy name, he thought as he was thrown forward, the seatbelt tightening across his chest.

A motorcyclist had cut in front of them and then inexplicably applied the brakes.

Adam added the lorry's normal road horn to the cacophony of sound.

An A to Z of South Essex street names landed on the engine cowling, thrown forward from its shelf on the bulkhead that separated the front of the cab from the rear.

Eddie replaced it.

Classy name, classy woman, maybe too classy for me, he thought, *but she gave me her card, and after a moment of cynicism, she softened, even smiled and what a smile.*

They saw the column of smoke before they saw the incident. A thick black plume rising straight into the autumn sky. At its base but standing clear was a young Freddie Muggins, who had neglected to tell the control staff when he phoned 999 that the reason his car was on fire was that he had driven into the back of a parked forty-foot trailer. The car and curtain sider were both well alight.

"Hey hey, here we go," said Adam.

Eddie picked up the hand mic, told control they were in attendance, and made pumps two.

6

"She's fit."

"Come again," asked Eddie.

"The female fireman," said Freddie Muggins.

The fire out, Eddie decided it was time to get the owners details. It irked him to hear comments like that, yet he couldn't explain why. Over the years, he had listen to hundreds of salacious comments from women about members of his crew and dealt with a few directed at himself, but this seemed different somehow.

"She's doing her job, so I'd appreciate it if you kept your thoughts to yourself."

"Sorry, mate, have I trod on your toes?"

"Just give me your details, pal."

Adam, Perry, and Ken were refilling their appliance's water tank from a fire hydrant. Jim Harris had finished sweeping the road and was placing the broom back on top of the rescue pump. Luke Dunstford was looking inside the burnt-out wreck. On the opposite pavement, Arthur Church was talking to a black police officer known by everyone as Dark Green. For years, Dark had worked in the traffic division with his white partner, with whom he shared the same surname, and who was, therefore, known as Light Green. They we're laughing, shoulder to shoulder. Eddie wanted to join them but felt it may be rude to interrupt what might be a private joke.

He placed his notebook inside his tunic and wandered over to Linsey Rivers. She had finished rolling the forty-five-millimetre hose and was placing it back in the locker.

"Why do they call the forty-five mill a bootlace, Guv?"

"You got me there, Linsey; might suggest it's easy to handle as opposed to the seventy mill. Anyway, your temporary transfer to us has been confirmed as permanent I hear. Happy?"

"Yes, Guv."

"Call me Eddie. Arthur's the guvner."

"Ok."

"Chris was also telling me how well you handled that job with the woman who wouldn't let us in. Well done."

Linsey ran the back of her hand across her brow, undid her tunic, and leant against the machine.

"Well, that's nice of Chris, but I'm not so sure, Eddie."

"Why?"

"She was scared when we got there and scared when we left. We done nuffin to help, might even have made it worse."

"How would we have made it worse?"

"She seemed genuinely in fear of us. I've been thinking of going back to see her."

"Hang on, Linsey. That ain't a good idea." It was Eddie's turn to open his tunic. It was Linsey's turn to ask why.

"You have a long career ahead of you. You're gonna step in and out of many lives."

"Yes, I know, and that's what I love."

Eddie continued, "Good, but you will have to attend to other people's pain. Some will have just lost their homes and everything they possess, or worse, their loved ones. There will be car smashes, industrial accidents, burns, scalds."

"Wow, you should be in recruitment."

"Very funny, ok, but witness it, don't embrace it. You do the job to the best of your ability, then walk away, otherwise, it will crush you."

"All the years you've done, Eddie. Never affected you?"

Eddie looked at the watch's latest recruit. Earlier this year, she had been in the same training squad as their last recruit, Sam, who had suffered life-changing injuries following a road traffic incident when he was struck by a motorcycle. He wanted to protect her.

He looked away.

The owner of the car was shouting into his mobile.

Two elderly women with their shopping trolleys stopped to wonder at the fire.

A sudden breeze chilled the sweat on his neck.

"It's incremental," he said.

He looked back at her.

"You have to handle it. Most of us have a job, a particular job, stuck in our brain, and it's not necessarily how long you have done. You could get something bad on your first day, but still, handle it you must."

"How?"

"Don't be afraid to talk, officially to a counsellor or this lot. They can appear to be a callous bunch."

"Tell me."

"They're not. It's all front. They understand."

"Graveyard humour can be harsh, but it's a pressure release valve. Don't be afraid to use it and use the other agencies, hotlines, etc., if you think someone needs help, but don't get involved, Linsey."

"Don't think she would appreciate other agencies, and if she found out it was me, I'm sure she would hate me."

"Oi, Lazy Rivers!" Luke strolled over. Linsey was the only member of the watch who was junior to him, and he wasn't going to let her forget it.

"'Ave ya made up the hose?"

Eddie thought of interrupting until Linsey replied.

"Yes, Puke, I've done it all as usual, and when we get back, you can make a nice cup of tea."

Luke looked at Eddie.

"Recruits these days, lippy as fuck."

Eddie looked at the two youngest members of the watch and was heartened by the bond that was being forged.

"See ya back at the ranch," he said, walking away.

7

Back at the ranch, it was stand easy. The term used for their mid-morning break. It consisted of a huge pot of tea that washed down rolls and baguettes filled with ham, cheese, and tuna mayo. Some preferred this to the lunchtime meal.

Jim picked up the tray of tea from the kitchen counter, and Adam grabbed the rolls.

Ken turned from the kitchen sink where he had just dropped a tea bag.

"There ya go, Linsey, your cup of Dip dang do dong."

"Thanks, Ken," said Linsey, taking the cup from him and adding a dash of milk.

Jim and Adam stopped.

"What was that?" Adam asked.

Linsey looked at them both and stirred.

"Lapsang souchong, it's a tea I like."

Jim ignored Linsey's remark. It was not her they were after.

"Can we have Lapsang do dong, Ken?"

"Linsey brings it in herself, alright, it's a black tea from China. Be lost on you two."

"Guys, help yourselves, I leave it in the dry goods cupboard."

Perry walked in and slammed his mess money on the counter. "Found it in my dirty overalls."

"And," said Ken.

"And what?"

Ken stared at Perry over his readers.

"Sorry."

"Thank you."

Harry Samuels joined the throng. His nickname was Harryoo, cos people's names were not his forte. He took a ham baguette off Adam's tray and a mug of tea off Jim's.

"This is nice, like a cocktail party."

Adam and Jim gave up and went over to the large mess table.

"Oh yea, Ken."

Harryoo continued.

"Shut up," said Perry under his breath.

"What?" Ken said.

Harryoo looked at Perry, not sure what his co-conspirator had just said before ploughing on regardless.

"Well, Ken, so as you know, I saw Perry give you his mess money last tour." Perry shook his head. Ken shook his head, and Linsey giggled.

Then, the bells went down.

8

Eddie got away sharp at the end of the day, keen to get a run in before the evening got too late and his workout affected his sleep. When he got home to his flat in Leigh on Sea, he stripped off, emptied his hold-all, and sorted his washing. Some went into the basket, some into the washing machine. He turned it on, went into the bedroom, and put on his running gear. He opened the doors to his balcony to experience the cold night air. It would be ok once he got going, no need for a warmer layer. He left his flat and made for the riverside via Gypsy Bridge. He had decided on the easy route along the promenade towards Southend Pier. It was flat as opposed to the other direction and the steep inclines of Belton Hills.

The dusky tide lapped the shore as he ran past Chalkwell Railway Station, where disgorging commuters from the city were eager for their homes. Other residents with much longer journeys were also arriving. The White Fronted Geese from Siberia, Grey Plover, and Oystercatchers to name but a few would overwinter in the estuary's marshes and reed beds where they were protected from mankind by the claggy sucking mud and the North Sea that the moon dragged up the river Thames into London.

Eddie was quickly into his stride. He was feeling good. He had read an article recently about one's biorhythms and how they influence one's physical, emotional and intellectual wellbeing. He didn't buy into it completely, but the way he was feeling tonight, all three cycles must be in the positive phase.

After the station, the path opens up onto the promenade proper. Other joggers were finishing their runs, some were turning intent on further punishment. Dogs, off their leads, cavorted on the beach now that summer was over.

Eddie began to sweat. He never wore headphones, preferring his own thoughts as he recycled his day.

It had been positive. Half a dozen shouts, all run of the mill and in between, he had time for all his paperwork that was now up-to-date. Arthur had relayed the amusing chat he'd had with Dark Green.

"I'd asked him where Light was."

"He's on leave and you can't call him Light anymore."

"How come?" Arthur had asked.

"He has passed his sergeant's exam. So, from now on, it's Bright Green." When they stopped laughing, Eddie told Arthur that while he was pleased to have Linsey on board, he was also concerned about not getting it right, having never worked alongside a woman, ever.

Arthur had sat back in his chair, pushed his glasses on his head, and said, "First off, I've contacted Leo Grant, as you know, now in charge of recruitment at HQ and asked for official guidance with regards to female recruits and any training packages for us all, which I seriously doubt they have. Secondly, don't worry, Eddie, you won't get it wrong because your intentions are good, plus I've spoken to Linsey a couple of times, officially like, and I think we have a good'un. What say you?"

Eddie was coming up to the Arches, a little row of bars and restaurants on the seafront at Westcliff. The barrelled caves once used by local fishermen for storage were now a popular oasis with excellent views of the estuary. He had frequented them more often in the past when he was a firefighter and this was his station's ground. An easy walk down the hill after work for a beer, then home.

Arthur had got it right as usual. Linsey was a firefighter, so treat her like one. What did her sex have to do with it?

Sex, he couldn't remember the last time.

He had been dating a French woman whom he met in Estuary English, a bar he favoured in Leigh, when his mother's accident happened.

He ran around a dog walker. The long lead took up half the prom.

Delphine, that was her name. She understood, said she'd wait, but he didn't understand. For a while, he understood nothing, how he was supposed to behave, what he was expected to say or do. His mother's unexpected demise consumed him. He never ended it, just ignored her, and despite the fact that she too lives in Leigh, he hadn't seen her since.

Not great, Eddie boy, he thought, jumping a saltwater puddle that had slopped over the sea wall from the recent high tide.

They dated, what, six times; there was no expectation, so he excused himself of any guilt.

Expectation, though, was exactly what he was experiencing now with Charlotte.

He ran through the nervous telephone conversation he'd had with her this afternoon. She sounded pleased to hear from him, her tone relaxed despite her formal office manner.

He had practised his opening line.

He wanted the timbre of his voice to be closer to George Clooney than George Formby.

Hi, Charlotte, it's me.

Hallo, Charlotte, it's Eddie.

Hallo, oh sod it.

He dialled her number.

While it rang, he paced back and forth across his room, then leant against his locker. He was about to hang up when she answered.

"Charlotte Barclay."

"Hallo, Eddie, it's me."

"Pardon."

"I mean Charlotte. Hallo, Charlotte, it's Eddie."

"Oh, hallo, Ed, thanks for phoning."

He moved the mouthpiece away and gave a sigh.

Then, feeling more confident, asked her how she was and how her day was going. He was surprised when she said boring.

"What about you, Eddie, rescued any damsels?"

There was a hard edge to her that unmanned him and exited him in equal measure. He imagined her turning away from her colleagues and smiling to herself.

"Just the three today."

"Ooh, tell me about it, sounds exciting."

"How about over dinner?"

"When?"

"Friday, I could come up town."

"Not Friday."

"Saturday?"

"Yes, I'll book the restaurant. This is my mobile number. Phone it, I'll send you the details. Got to go, bye."

He looked at his phone, placed it on his desk, and sat down.

The conversation lasted, what, two minutes? *Two minutes that might change my life*, he thought, rubbing his chin. She was nonchalant, playful, and assertive, quite a lot to pack into two minutes, and there it was again, the delicate stomach punch when she called him Ed. Only one other woman abbreviated his name down to two letters, one syllable, Jane.

One time, almost a member of his family. Jane and his mother, Eve, shared a close bond. Jane's daughter, Charlotte, honoured Eve's encouragement by taking a place at Reading University. Over the years, Eddie would go to Jane's salon. Jane would cut his hair and listen to his day, his problems, his grief.

Jane was his childhood sweetheart and had been his emotional lodestar, but Jane was married to big Nev, and there is only so much any man would accept regarding the relationship his wife could have with another man. Consideration also had to be given that a right-hander from Nev would put you in intensive care.

Eddie had reached Southend Pier. The self-styled longest pleasure pier in the world. During the Victorian era, paddle steamers ferried Londoners to Margate and Ramsgate, bypassing Southend because at low tide, the sea is more than a mile out. The town was missing out on the tourist trade. A London mayor and the business elite, all too aware of the saying that if the mountain will not come to Mohammed, build an elevated railway out to sea. His mother often walked him as a child to the end of the pier before they rode the train back.

"Breath it in, Son, breath in that fresh salty air." They would stop, halfway, and sit in a wooden shelter thickly painted for weather protection so she could smoke a cigarette. He would watch men fish and look back along the undulating coastline to Leigh, where one day he would live. He had come to terms with his loss but still missed her. Turning to start his homeward run, he knew he always would.

9

Charlie Rivers threw a couple of steaks on the barbecue. The burgers, sausages, and chicken breasts were in the warming cabinet, all cooked to perfection. The two ribeye steaks were for his sons. The only members of his family who shared his passion for beef. He had prepped them with a salt and pepper rub and would serve them medium rare. He breathed in the succulent aroma as the marbled cuts sang to him on the grill. High cholesterol deprived him of his favourite food these days unless it was a special occasion. As lovely as it was to have the family round for some mid-week scoff, it didn't qualify as significant; plus, his wife, Ange, would be on his case if she saw anything other than a chicken breast accompanying his salad.

Inside the house, Angela had gathered the family around the table and insisted that the football be turned off. Places at the table, though never discussed, were always the same. Charlie would be at the end, nearest to the patio doors. He referred to it as the head of the table.

"Oh yea," said Ange, "so what's my end?"

"Your end is lovely, darling," was the reply.

On either side of Charlie sat his sons, Mark and Howard. Mark was the eldest and ran Charlie's second butcher shop. He had learnt the trade from his father and was confident that one day, he would be at the helm of the small but successful family business.

Howard was an accountant and second in line to the throne. He specialised in tax law and the London firm he worked for was considered the best in giving advice to multi-nationals on how to reduce the curse to a bare minimum. Charlie admired the dedication Mark had to their shops and his tireless work ethic, but knew the few hours Howard gave him on tax advice were just, if not more, valuable.

The chef came in from the garden and placed a platter of meat in the middle of the table.

"Brr...getting chilly out there. Tuck in, everyone."

Linsey waited for her sisters-in-law to help themselves before taking a burger. "Is that it, love?"

"Yes, Mum, big meal lunch time."

"How is the food at the station, Lins?" Howard shouted down the table.

"Yea, good. Ken does an excellent job."

"You have a chef, nice," said Michelle, Howard's wife.

She placed some salad on her plate, then leant across the crib where her daughter nestled and handed the bowl to Linsey.

Linsey laughed. "He's not a chef, he's one of the watch, a firefighter."

"Maybe it's a job you could do, Linsey, instead of putting out fires," said Nancy.

Nancy flicked at her long black hair and teased her centre parting. She had her hand on Mark's knee while glancing a look across the table at Howard. Angela pushed out a small pout with her lips as she poured herself a glass of water and worried if the subconscious flirtation was for the right son.

"You should have some salad, Bradley." Angela held the bowl out to her grandson.

He shook his head, placing a sausage in a soft white roll.

"It's good for you," she persisted.

"It's ok, Angela, he had baked beans with his lunch." Nancy shot her sullen ten-year-old a glance.

"Don't get sauce on your shirt."

Linsey often wondered what her brother saw in Nancy. A loud, self-centred, vacuous woman who constantly sought attention and had little time for Bradley, her introverted son. Apart from that, she was ok. Linsey smiled to herself.

"Alright, love?"

"Yea, Mum, just er...thinking back to something earlier today."

"C'mon, share it, little sis," said Mark, leaning over his plate to stick a pink irregular cut of beef in his mouth.

Nancy touched her earring, revealing a small tattoo of a heart on the underside of her wrist. She looked at Linsey. "Oh, please, Linsey, do tell." Linsey held her cutlery as taught by her mother, desperate to instil a modicum of elegance in her daughter. She trapped the rocket salad between her knife and fork. The delicate manoeuvre was incongruous for such abrasive hands and dirty fingernails. She thought fast.

"Well, I took some Lapsang Souchong into work."

Howard held up his tea mug.

"Perfect with a steak," he said.

"Nearly as good as this beer," said his brother.

'Hands of stone', her father used to say as he parried his daughter's childhood punches.

She was at the point in her tale when Ken mispronounced the name of the tea. Expecting to hear a ripple of laughter around the table, she looked up from her plate and saw her bemused family staring at her.

"Dip dang do dong," she repeated slowly. She coloured a lighter pink than her brother's food.

"It was funny at the time."

"Yea, I can see why you chose that profession, Sis," said Mark, swigging his beer. "We up for golf this weekend, Bruv?"

"I think so. What about you, Dad?" Howard asked. The three men went into their own conversation.

Michelle leant over the crib and pulled the cover below her daughter's chin. "Ange was saying you sleep in the same room as the men, Linsey."

"Dormitory, yea."

"It's not right, is it, Michelle?"

Angela was indignant on her daughter's behalf.

Michelle took more salad.

"Little bit?"

She asked her young nephew sitting opposite.

Bradley shook his head.

"A tomato, one little tomato."

He nodded his consent.

"I don't know if I'd be comfortable with it; Howard wouldn't."

"It's a large room and the beds are partitioned off from one another."

"But still," said her mother.

"We are not all naked, top and tailed in one large bed, Mum."

This piqued Nancy's interest.

"So, when you all jump up in the middle of the night to go to something…"

"A shout."

"You shout?"

"It's called a shout."

Nancy shook her head and continued.

"Anyway, you all jump up to put on your clothes."

"I presume lights come on," said Michelle.

"Emergency lighting." Linsey was beginning to enjoy the interest being shown in her job, albeit the more prosaic aspect of it.

Nancy's salacious imagination had been sparked into life and she wasn't letting go the thought in her head.

"So, all the lights come on, you all jump up half naked, well you must see certain things, sometimes?"

"Exactly. Bradley, go and watch TV, love," said Angela as she bit the end of her breadstick.

"What things?" Linsey asked, toying with them.

"You know…" Nancy nodded to an imaginary crotch. "Men, in the morning."

"Any swollen members of the watch?"

"Michelle!" Angela exclaimed reaching for the wine.

Linsey and Michelle giggled. Nancy, eyes agog, awaited her answer.

"We sleep in tee shirts pants, and socks, our overall trousers laid out on the floor next to the bed. The bells go down. Sit up, sling your legs out, slide into your trousers, slip your shoes on, and out to the lorries. Seconds, and no, sorry, haven't seen a thing."

Linsey pierced a radish, then continued.

"Well, I ain't yet and having lived most of my life in this house with them three down there roaming around half naked, fighting with bath towels, farting and belching, it wouldn't be the biggest shock of my life."

Angela nodded in agreement. She had to concede that point.

Nancy turned back to the men and her glass of Malbec.

"Is it difficult, Lins, jumping up like that when you're soundo?" Her nicer sister-in-law asked.

"Depends, Michelle. If you are soundo, you know in a deep sleep, then yea. You can wake up and wonder where you are and what's going on. Otherwise, it's ok. What I don't like is you jump up, the adrenaline is pumping, you go quickly to the bay, not crazy like, and it's not your lorry going out. You're pumped but for nothing."

"Can you get back to sleep?"

"Well, I don't know if the others have noticed but I go in the gym and do press ups, ten, twenty just to get rid of the adrenaline, then I go back to the dorm, turn on my night light, and read."

"Interesting," said Michelle looking at her baby.

Angela looked up the other end of the table as her husband was reaching out with his fork for the last burger.

"Charlie Rivers!"

He sat back with a sigh.

10

Eddie came through his front door. He prised off his trainers without undoing the laces. He put his keys on the small hook by the coat rack, then wiping his palms on the back of his shorts, picked up his phone from the console table. His father had phoned. His father never phoned, ever. Ray had lived in a time when the call box at the end of the street was for emergencies. Friends were met on a Friday night in the club, visitors called on Sunday afternoons. Idle gossip was like charity, a waste of time. Everyone's largesse let the governments of the world off the hook and as far as he was concerned, that's how the phone could stay. So, with a degree of reluctance, he had accepted a mobile phone from his son when he had moved back to London.

"What for?"

"Just in case and this is how you use it. Keep it charged up."

Eddie called immediately. He went into his kitchen and with some paper towel, started to wipe sweat from his neck and forehead.

The phone rang for an anxious minute that seemed much longer. "Dad."

"Hallo, Son."

"You ok?"

"Yea, I'm alright."

"You phoned."

"Yea, I've broken my wrist."

"So, you're not alright. How did it happen?"

"Tripped over the bloody rug in the lounge. Slipper caught the edge and I went arse over elbow."

Eddie thoughts were tumbling over one another trying to get to the front of the queue.

"How bad is it? Are you in plaster? Is it painful?"

Ray tidied up the questions and replied, "I've been to A&E, I'm in plaster, and I'm not in pain, they gave me tablets. They are making me drowsy." He added, "I'm going to bed."

Eddie's thoughts started to behave.

"Ok, keep your phone by your bed and phone me if you need help, doesn't matter what time. I'll be up tomorrow night. Can you feed yourself until I get there?"

"Yea, Meena has made me a curry."

Eddie assumed Meena was a neighbour; it didn't matter for now.

"I'll be up tomorrow after work."

Linsey lay on her bed, hands behind her head, staring at the ceiling with a book on her chest. She shared a house in St Viviers Road with three of her girlfriends. Along this elegant thoroughfare of large detached houses, a fight was ensuing between the older middle class desperate to maintain the grandeur of the single-family home and the gradual slide into bed sit land. Linsey's place occupied a plot at the nicer end near the small park, much to the dismay of the families that surrounded it.

Linsey never understood why the neighbours cold shouldered her and her mates. They had friends over but never partied hard, kept the place clean and tidy, and Linsey cut the grass, though not it's edges. The windows needed cleaning and the drapes in the living room window never fitted properly, leaving gaps when drawn. It wasn't a palace, it wasn't a doss house.

Linsey was the first to leave her parents' house this evening, making an excuse about a busy day tomorrow. She could imagine the conversation that took place about her job following her departure.

Her brothers would display a mild indifference, as they always had to their little sister. Nancy would search for a trite remark, give up, and hope her sad expression conveyed her sympathy to her parents-in-law.

Michelle would be supportive, even thinking her brave. Her mother, ignoring all comments, would convey her worry, even though she wasn't exactly sure what to worry about. Her dad would remain silent.

Linsey shared his quiet determination, resolved to plough her own furrow. She recalled the conversation she had with him when joining the service.

"Of course, you will handle it, darling. Between you, me, and the gatepost, I've often thought you are tougher than your brothers."

"When you were kids, mum would bring you to the shop sometimes on the way home from school. Mark always wanted to chop the meat. I'd place a cleaver in his hand and hold his wrist while he brought it down on a piece of scrag end I had for the dog. Howard always hung back, staying close to his mother's skirt. On this particular day, you were squatting on your haunches, running your fingers through the sawdust on the floor. A line of blood ran off the chopping block and onto your bare arm. You looked at it, then at me. I tried to maintain a neutral pose, awaiting your reaction."

"I don't remember that, Dad. Did I scream the place down?"

"No, love, you picked up a handful of sawdust and wiped it across your arm. Then, you stood and wandered back to your mother and this makes me laugh to this day. While she was speaking to Ernie—remember him, worked for us for years—you wiped your hands on her dress. You'll be fine."

She knew her constitution was strong and her father's support and mum's natural concern, all wrapped in love, made it cast-iron. It's what we all need. It's the power behind the first step out the door every day.

So, what power did Patricia Arnold have? A woman is scared to open the door. It had been troubling Linsey since that day in the woman's kitchen. Eddie was right, she mustn't take on the woes of the world, provide good counsel, right the wrongs, but she felt sure Patricia Arnold needed the support that she took for granted.

Despite her harsh exterior, Patricia's arms embraced a frightened heart and her eyes revealed her troubled mind.

So, prior to her family dinner, Linsey drove to the house of Patricia Arnold. She parked at a discreet distance and took out her phone with the pretence of making a call.

In the TV programmes, they staked out a joint for hours, days. Linsey would give it fifteen minutes and hope that within that brief window, she would see coming and going of a man perhaps, or Patricia with a man and they would be larking about, having fun as they slammed the front door and sauntered off to the pub. Something positive to belay her fears.

After twenty minutes, she put her phone away and thought how stupid this idea had been. Then, she saw her.

She was walking slowly down the street with a young boy in tow. The child was a reluctant companion, pulling back to make it as hard for Patricia as he could. A sea anchor in stormy weather. She stopped and leant over the child.

Linsey could only guess of what she said. Some frustrated cajoling to attain the kid's compliance. Instead, he tried kicking her, and the slow progress resumed.

Linsey wanted to get out and say, 'Hi, I was just passing', but knew at this stressful moment, she would have been greeted in a similar vein to their initial meeting.

Patricia got to the gate, wedged open against uneven concrete, and the boy ran down the path and jumped on the doorstep, raising his arms in triumph. As the beleaguered woman arrived in second place, Linsey saw the logo emblazoned on the back of her fleece. It was a local supermarket chain, the one Linsey had passed on the way to her stakeout. As the door closed on the squabbled life of Patricia Arnold, Linsey's next move took shape in her mind.

11

The water tender made its way across town displaying blues while not sounding the twos. It was a silent approach for a person of a troubled mind on the roof of a flat block, who could be spooked into jumping by the wailing two tones. A personal agony ended by the would-be saviours.

The summer, hot and dry, had not pleased the trees of Langden. They were shedding their leaves in a blatant show of their displeasure: 'Look what you made us do'. The horse chestnut had led the protest in late August, dropping its payload of conkers. The fruit, once collected for munitions because of the cordite it contains, lay unwontedly about. The younger generation of the town, forsaking ancient games for electronic devices, were uninterested. The ash, beach, and cherry were following suit. The result of the abscission collected in gutters, ran along kerbsides, and blocked the storm drains, or spiralled upwards in mini tornadoes as the fire appliance swept past.

Before the bells went down, Eddie had been talking to Clarence Siddall. Clarence was the assistant divisional officer in charge of Langden Fire Station. Eddie had clocked him going into his office, so grabbing two mugs of tea off the aluminium tray, he followed him.

Clarence had taken off his number one jacket, placed it over a hanger, then hung it on the coat stand next to the photograph of Prince Andrew.

Clarence was staring intently at Her Majesty's favourite when he was joined by Eddie.

"Tea?"

"Hi, Eddie, thanks."

The two men stood side by side and sipped their hot beverages.

Both considered the artwork.

Clarence was the first to speak.

"It's like working with a bunch of juveniles."

"I don't know, it's well executed," replied Eddie.

A person or persons unknown had chinagraphed a pair of sunglasses onto the official photograph of the senior royal.

"You have a point," said Clarence, who had decided to get in sync with Eddie's humour.

"What do you think, Ray Ban?"

Eddie nodded. "Wayfarer definitely."

"Anyone on your watch?"

"No, not us, Guv, we're all abstract impressionists."

Clarence sat behind his desk.

"New hobby now, cos your football days are over?"

"What?"

"Art appreciation."

"No, no." Eddie was keen to change the subject.

"I wanted to know if you knew Sean Stolly; he joins us on nights."

"Yea, I know him. Sit down if you're stopping. We were at Colchester together. Different Watches, so I don't know him really well."

Clarence sipped. "What can I say? Seemed popular, two commendations, union man, which will please Arthur."

"Oh, come on, Arthur's not that shallow."

"Alright, please you then."

"Thanks."

"I thought a couple of your lot know him?"

"Yea, they do, but I just get the usual, he's alright."

Eddie sat.

"I did hear he was called moss at training school, referring to, evidently, how it grows on the north side of a tree; shady."

"I know a few people that epithet could apply to."

Clarence smiled, then turned to look out the window at the constant stream of soundless traffic.

Eddie knew Clarence well enough to know more was to come. He waited. "Do you remember, a good few years ago now, five, six, seven maybe, Anne Widdecombe said of Michael Howard, I think he was the home secretary at the time, that he had something of the night about him." He turned back to Eddie.

"Yea, I remember, not sure I know what it means, though."

"Nor do I," said Clarence.

"Ok, thanks for the insight."

"When I say I don't know what it means, I mean it's hard to put into words, more like a feeling—intuitive—if you get my drift."

"Yea, I get it."

Eddie glanced up at Prince Andrew. Eddie thought the shades improved the visage. He was reminded of any establishment figure, especially politicians, when trying to look cool looked the opposite. He conjured an image of Prince Charles in double denim and white trainers.

"Why don't you lock the office when you're not here?"

"Oh, and set 'em a real challenge? They'd love that."

Now as Eddie booked in attendance, he began to appreciate the profundity of Clarence's remark and hoped it did not bode ill for the watch.

The four-storey flat block was located in a pedestrian precinct. Adam parked the lorry on the hard standing provided for emergency vehicles and stayed behind the wheel. Eddie, Perry, and Linsey walked across the crunchy, hay-coloured grass to where the police officers who had asked for the presence of the fire service stood. They were looking up, as were the kids on bikes just home from school, a couple of teenagers who'd swerved education this day and a few pissed off residents of the adjacent maisonettes who longed for a bit of peace a quiet. The people on this estate lived cheek by jowl. In hot weather, much of that living took place in gardens and on the streets; now, it had spread to the roofs. A step too far for the law-abiding majority.

Eddie said hallo to the police officers.

When you rock up at an incident, it's good to be apprised of the situation by the emergency service already in attendance. This occasion needed no such information. The man on the roof was not of a suicidal nature, more of a cornered animal defiant in the face of the odds. He paced along the flat roof like a caged tiger waiting to be fed.

"We were giving chase until…" The copper pointed up.

"What's he done?" Perry asked.

The copper shook his head. "Never you mind," he said.

"How has he got up there?" Eddie asked.

It was the turn of the female police officer.

"Can you believe that at the top of those stairs is a roof hatch secured by a simple sliding bolt? Unbelievable."

The central staircase was open to the elements, serving the flats on either side of it.

"The last thing we were gonna do was follow him…" She emphasised the male pronoun. "Up there."

"You put a fucking ladder up, Mr Fireman, and I'm jumping. I tell ya, I'll fucking jump."

The tiger had clocked the fire crews below.

"The ALP has arrived, Eddie," said Linsey.

"Can you help?" The male copper asked.

"Give us a minute," said Eddie. He wanted to talk to Chris, who was riding in charge of the Ariel Ladder Platform. Harryoo was driving.

As Eddie walked over to where the ALP had parked directly behind the water tender, he was joined by one of the residents from the maisonettes. The tiger maintained the tirade.

"Put up a fucking ladder, Mr Fireman, and I'm jumping."

The elderly man in a pure white vest and grey flannel trousers held up by dark blue braces had a plea for Eddie, who was obviously in charge.

"Do us all a favour, mate, and put up your bloody ladder."

Linsey sidled over to the female police officer who had strolled a few yards from her partner. The two boys on their bikes looked at her and asked if she was a real fireman.

"No, got the uniform from that fancy dress shop in the town centre."

"Should have got one that fitted."

"Clear off, you two," said the copper.

"We live here."

"What's your names?"

They peddled away.

"My dad said when he was a kid, if you were lippy to a policeman, you got a clip around the ear."

"Can't touch the little darlings now."

"Linsey," she said, introducing herself.

"Chloe."

"I'm trying to imagine how he got through the roof hatch," said Linsey.

"Up onto the bannister, slid the bolt, and pulled himself through. I think kicking me in the shoulder helped his upward trajectory." Chloe rotated her arm slightly.

"So, I'm looking forward to nicking this one."

"Do you think he knew about the hatch or just got lucky, so to speak?"

"His type knows every unlocked hatch, gate and door. Not lucky, just stupid." The tiger noticed Linsey and Chloe looking up.

The two women in their lumpen uniforms were the epitome of everything he despised—representatives of State, of oppression, of control.

Of don't.

Don't speed here; don't light it there; don't drink in the town; don't enjoy a late-night fry-up.

Servants to the establishment from his own class. Fucking bitch traitors. He would fuck both of them. Fuck some sense into them, especially the blonde fire girl. Yea, he'd fuck her. With one hand, he grabbed his crotch, and the other made a 'V' sign over his mouth, through which his tongue protruded.

"His mother loves him," said Chloe.

Linsey wondered.

"You done this long?" Linsey asked.

"Five years. You?"

"Five minutes. Do you mind me asking if you found, find it difficult, you know, in a male-dominated environment?"

"No, I don't mind. Us police girls been around longer than you fire girlies, so it's more accepted, but fight your corner is all I'd say. Don't take any crap. You finding it tough?"

"No, no, I work with a great bunch, just wanted to, you know."

Chloe gave her a sideways glance as Linsey blushed.

"Well, good for you. I work with a bunch of wankers."

"Really!"

Chloe attempted a smile, then thought better of it.

"I told dopey draws there not to request you, but he wouldn't listen."

"Why?"

"Cos you won't do anything. So, it's a waste of your time."

Linsey noticed Perry starting to walk over to them.

Please don't, she thought. *I don't want this conversation interrupted.*

"Like I said, I've been in five minutes. Why do you think we won't help?" Chloe pointed to the ALP.

"The Ariel Platform, right?"

Linsey nodded.

"You are not putting that up alongside that roof because numb nuts up there ain't coming quietly, and if you think you're taking me up there onto a flat roof with no guard rail to arrest an aggressive man, well, you've got another thing coming. Even dopey draws ain't that dopey. Your Subby, Eddie, ain't it?"

"Yea, Eddie Hart."

"Is he married?"

"No."

The question threw Linsey for a second, wondering what it had to do with this situation.

"Why?"

"Just wondered. Anyway, he knows that and I bet that's the conversation he's having right now with the officer in charge of the platform."

Perry arrived at the same time as a special constable.

Everyone said, "Alright."

"What do you need, Chloe?"

"Go and park your arse on the top landing. The last thing we need is him attempting entry into one of those top flats. Then, we would have a siege on our hands."

"Will do."

The three watched the eager young special take on the stairs two at a time. "So what now?" was Linsey's final question.

"Well, I reckon it's a 'thanks for coming but leave it with us'. We have another car coming, so we will stand here drinking tea, hopefully." Chloe glanced at the neighbours at their front doors.

"He will start getting cold and finally realise that he has fucked up."

"Then what?" Perry asked.

"I reckon he'll make some stupid demand like, 'I want a solicitor'. We will say 'Ok, mate, of course'."

"Then what?" Linsey echoed. It was definitely her last question.

"Then, when he drops onto the landing, I'm nicking him," and with that thought in mind, she smiled.

So, the charade had a few more hours to play out, minus the Red Watch, who had wended their way home. Linsey drove the water tender. She had been a driver before joining the service. Van driver and, more importantly, a bus driver, so only required a three-day conversion course to drive fire appliances. Her pump operating skills were learnt at training school, so she now only needed some hours of practice in handling an emergency vehicle.

She reversed the lorry off the hard standing with Adam and Perry seeing her back. Having someone at the rear of the appliance when reversing is de rigueur. An accident without lookouts is a chargeable offence. Back on the road, Adam and Perry jumped in the rear of the cab.

"Thanks, lads."

It was the required etiquette. She was about to pull away when she noticed the boys who had lipped her earlier. They had watched in awed silence as she manoeuvred the large, noisy beast onto the roadway.

Linsey wound down her window.

"See ya, boys."

They nodded.

"And be good."

She gave them a thumbs up.

One responded with the same sign and the other waved.

"Where to, Eddie?"

"Go up onto the dual carriageway where you can put your foot down, then back via the industrial park that's always busy. See how you handle heavy traffic."

At the top of the on-slip, she picked up speed to match the flow of traffic and to ease in where appropriate.

Adam and Perry stood in the rear, looking over the bulkhead that divides the cab.

Linsey was conscious of the three pairs of eyes evaluating her driving, but also knew it was inevitable.

Eddie, also conscious of it, broke the ice.

"A guvner I had years ago said to me, learn something from every job you go to, no matter how small. Although we didn't do anything, what did you learn from that incident, Linsey?"

"Don't trap yourself on a roof when escaping from plod."

"Try to hide in the bushes."

Eddie ignored the trite remarks from behind him.

Linsey was smiling as she checked her mirrors.

"Well, Eddie, I was wondering why the police called us in the first place because…" She then proceeded to repeat verbatim what Chloe's take on it was, finishing with, "So they will wait it out and he'll come down when he's cold."

Her in-depth analysis impressed a quietude on the three men, until, "Should have overtaken the tractor earlier," said Perry.

"Yea, stuck behind a slow-moving vehicle now," added Adam.

12

After work, Eddie jumped in his car and headed against the flow of traffic into London. Arthur still had contacts in his old brigade and had arranged parking for Eddie at Dowgate. There was none at his father's. The fire station on Upper Thames Street is at the base of a large office building and could easily be missed when navigating the busy thoroughfare. Eddie parked on the front apron and rang the doorbell. He waited, wondering how many pranksters, drunks, and idiots did the same thing. He held up his ID card by way of introduction as the door opened.

"Hallo, Eddie Hart. I'm a sub in Essex. My boss phoned up about parking."

"Oh yea, saw it in the handing over book. You ok there on the front apron?"

"Well, I might be here for a couple of days."

"Ok, I'll let you through the bay. Park right at the back of the drill yard out of the way."

Eddie walked passed the Tower of London, lit by floodlights, and imagined living there, protected by the thousand-year-old walls. Arthur had told him that if you asked to go to the church service in there on a Sunday morning, the Yeoman guard had to let you in gratis.

The night was cool and dry. The river, at rest on high tide, lapped gently against the bridge before turning once again in its Sisyphean task towards the sea.

A group of young women and men dressed for a night out and pre-loaded with drinks approached him. Each woman carried a champagne flute. As they approached Eddie, one stumbled on the cobblestone and dropped her glass. "Whey!" The men cheered.

"Bollocks, I'd only had one mouthful."

"Don't worry, I'll get you another mouthful later, darling," said one of the men, grabbing her around the waist as the general response to his comment rose to a crescendo. They stumbled on, leaving the shards of glass for someone else to clear up.

Eddie wondered how much more glassware had the same fate in store for it tonight.

He had maybe a mile and a half to walk to his father's place near Hermitage Basin in Wapping. The exercise was good, and the route was far from boring. New property was springing up, and old warehouses were being converted in the gentrification of a once notorious area.

"Hallo, Dad."

"In 'ere, Son."

Eddie hung his coat, noticing for the first time the three black and white framed prints on the hall wall.

Ray was sitting in front of the telly. In front of him on the low stool was a shallow wooden tray containing a greasy plate and spoon. The narrow wooden sides of the tray reminded Eddie of his time at sea. The fiddles that could be raised on the ship's tables in rough weather to prevent the crockery from sliding off. The room smelled spicy.

"Another curry, Dad?"

Ray's son picked up the tray and headed for the kitchen.

"You know it has never been my favourite food, but those dishes from Meena are delicious."

"Want anything?"

"Water, please, got a tablet to take." Eddie returned with a glass and handed it to his father.

"Thanks."

Ray placed it on the floor and reached into his pocket for a small bottle of pills.

He offered them to Eddie.

"Would you?"

Eddie read the label, twisted off the cap, and shook one out onto his palm.

"There ya go."

"You didn't have to come up, Son, I can manage."

"Looks like it," said his son, replacing the cap.

"I got Meena opposite and Colm upstairs; between the three of us, we have it covered. Thanks, though."

"What does Colm do?"

"Bit of fetch and carry, anything I want, really."

"Does he give you a knock?"

"Yea, or I phone him. Handy these mobiles."

The two men looked at one another, enjoying what was never going to be, a lost remark.

"Well, it was obvious I was coming up, but if I'm honest, it would do me a favour to crash here for a night or two."

"Ah, ulterior motive."

"More like two birds with one stone."

"Well, if I'm the old crow, who's the turtle dove?"

Eddie smiled.

"More like a wise old owl, I think."

He sat in the middle of the sofa and spread his arms and legs in an expansive mood as he looked around the room.

"Those black and white photographs in the hall. Haven't seen them before."

"Don't change the subject, tell me about the bird and I'll tell you about them."

Eddie became embarrassed, this was a conversation he had never had with his father. A man who, for most of Eddie's upbringing, was a spectre and, when he was around, a cold, elusive third party in his and his mother's lives. Ray knew Jane when Eddie had brought her home from school, and of her marriage to Nev and their daughter, Charlotte, but any adult relationships Eddie had would have gone unnoticed. Now, he was on the verge of confiding to his father his albeit initial thoughts about a woman.

Eddie sat forward on the edge of the sofa and rested his arms on his knees. "Last time I was here, I went to the National Gallery, remember, to see the painting."

"The Turner, yea, I remember."

"Did you know the painting, Dad, before that day, that article?"

"Of course, Son."

Since his mother's tragic death, it was as if Eddie had discovered a photo album long hidden of his father's life. Each page turned did not reveal past happiness but new revelations.

"Well, I met her there. She works there, research."

Ray held his broken wrist trying to find a comfortable point of rest. "What's her name?"

"Charlotte, Charlotte Barclay." Eddie liked to say it aloud.

"She sounds sophisticated."

"Yes, Dad. I can't say I know her that well, probably punching."

"Well, Son, if anyone can punch above their weight, you can."

"Thanks, Dad. What about those photos?"

"When you seeing her?"

"Tomorrow evening for dinner. Photos?"

"They're mine."

"What, you took them?"

"Yea. Taken black and white for years."

"I never saw any evidence of that at home."

"Never brought any of it back to Stanford. Phylis kept all my equipment in her place."

Ray had a long-term relationship with Phylis that only came to light this year. Just like his mother's death, this had been another blow Eddie had to come to terms with.

"Why not, Dad?"

Ray stood and looked at the rug, a cream-coloured rectangle.

"I'd better get rid of that before I break the other wrist. Want it?"

"Don't know, Dad."

Ray looked at the lean, good-looking man sitting on his sofa and found it hard to believe he was his progeny. How could he have spent a lifetime so uninterested in this fine man? A superb gift bestowed yet unappreciated.

He felt lightheaded and sat quickly on the chair by the table.

"You ok, Dad?"

"Yea, pass me the water, would you?"

He sipped until the feeling passed. Eddie sat across the table from his father. "Earlier this year, Son, I told you everything and yet I told you nothing. The one argument, the one conversation we had, would never contain a lifetime. I stayed with your mother out of duty, but all those weekends up here in London, so many weekends, that was another life, and, though it pains you to hear it, Son, that was my life."

"You know, as soon as I got to Phylis' house, the first thing I always done was change my clothes. I never cross-contaminated. So, no, I never brought a camera home."

Eddie looked down at the rug and wondered where he could put it.

"I saw a counsellor for a while, Dad. Jane suggested it and it paid dividends coming to terms with things; not just you and me, but everything. I remember mum saying, 'Take a positive from a negative whenever you can, sunshine'".

"So, I know there may be further revelations, and if so, I'll look upon them with surprise, not despair, Dad."

Father and son looked across the table at one another.

"Unless you're a serial killer."

13

Sitting centrally below the apex of the roof, the supermarket's red and yellow logo, designed as a sunburst to brighten everyone's day, shone out against the black cladding.

An elderly woman was struggling to free a trolley from its indistinguishable cousin until a young mother, eager to put her youngest in a basket seat, came to her aid. She called to her other child, who sat in the coin-operated helicopter, to follow as the front doors of the shop slid open. Two men stood shaking buckets while another suggested breakdown recovery service should be considered. All three were ignored.

Linsey was on another stakeout. She was sure this was Patricia Arnold's place of work. The logo on her fleece matched the shop sign, and it was walking distance from her house. What she didn't know was if Patricia was at work.

Linsey had been woken early by a group of raucous gulls.

Must be a union meeting, she thought, pulling open her curtains to see them dive bombing kebab road kill.

Her Saturday was overshadowed by the coming night shift starting at 1800 hours, so no lunchtime drinks with her housemates. Obviously, there were plenty of mundane tasks requiring her attention, but they couldn't be done on a weekend. No, mundane was meant for mid-week. The weekend required imagination, so here she was, outside this shop, trying to imagine how she could make contact with Patricia Arnold if only to say, 'Is everything ok, can I help?'.

The confidence she had in her bedroom had evaporated as her thoughts see-sawed between going into the shop and going home. She looked at the car park sign that told her she had two hours. She had been sitting there in her car for thirty-five minutes.

"Make a decision, Lins," she said aloud.

She needed to use a toilet. So, it was decided. Go in, use the loo, and see what happens.

Eddie was up and making breakfast while his father was in the bathroom. He could hear Ray swearing.

He plated up the food, poured the tea, and then went to the bathroom door.

"You alright, Dad?"

"What do you bloody think?"

Eddie's smile was quickly curtailed when the door swung open.

"You ever tried wiping your arse with the wrong hand?" They sat at the table with the food in front of them.

Eddie started to eat, then realised why his father was staring at his breakfast. "Sorry, Dad, not much of a nurse, eh?"

Eddie started cutting Ray's food up.

Ray reached for a slice of toast from the stack of four.

"Here, let me," said Eddie, beating him to it. He didn't fancy Ray's maladroit hand anywhere near his food.

"What time are you off out today?"

"Later this afternoon, Dad. I thought I'd make you a stew before I went."

"Nice."

"You?"

"I might have a walk down by the river."

"Did you know you can ask to go to church in the tower on a Sunday morning, and they have to let you in."

"Yea, and they'll march you straight out afterwards, Son. They have been guarding that place for seven centuries, they ain't that gullible."

"Good point."

Eddie swigged his tea.

"Your birthday is not that far off, Dad. I wondered if you fancied a small coffee machine?"

"When have you ever seen me drink coffee?"

"I just thought."

"I was hoping for cast cast-iron balti dish."

Eddie swallowed his sausage prematurely and coughed.

"Really!"

Ray started to chuckle.

"Are you really an officer, in charge of people?" He asked before catching his broken wrist on the edge of the table.

"Ow! Jesus Christ."

The two breakfasts started to congeal until the two men stopped laughing and gathered their composure.

Linsey jinked through the crowd of people and into the shop. The toilets were normally at the back, out of the way. As she turned into the dry goods aisle, she saw Patricia Arnold stacking shelves. Linsey stopped and pretended to search for a product on the stand in front of her. It was now or never.

Breathing deep, she wiped her palms down the side of her jeans, then made her way towards her.

"Excuse me, can you tell me where the toilets are, please?"

Patricia turned and, with a false smile, said they were out of order, vandalised.

"Thanks, typical, eh?"

"Sorry, love."

Linsey turned to go when her see-saw of bravery went from bottom to top.

"Say you're Patricia, right? Patricia Arnold?"

Patricia returned to her job.

"Might be. Who wants to know?"

"I thought I recognised you. I'm Linsey. I was at your house the other day."

"At my house." The knuckles holding the tin can turned white.

"Yea, that little incident the…"

Linsey lowered he voice as a customer passed.

"The fire."

Patricia turned again.

Linsey watched the false bonhomie fade completely. It was replaced by a delicate tic under Patricia's left eye. She nodded slowly.

"Well, as I said, weren't a fire so."

"Everything ok now? Get a new bowl for the sink?"

Linsey tried to sound lighthearted.

"You live around here?"

"No, I was just passing and…"

Linsey hesitated.

"Saw the shop, needed a pee. Know how it is."

"Yea, I know how it is. Thanks for asking."

Linsey couldn't think where to take the conversation. She looked along the aisle to a toddler in its stroller. His older brother got up from lying on the floor and stuck a hand in the youngster's mouth.

"Natural inoculation," she said aloud.

"Pardon."

"Oh, nothing as long as you are ok. You are, right?"

"Like I said, thanks for asking."

Patricia Arnold held a steely gaze.

"Well, it was nice to see you, take care."

Linsey walked out of the store feeling foolish. Why didn't she take Eddie's advice? Halfway to her car, she felt a tap on her shoulder. She turned to be confronted by an angry woman. Patricia Arnold had followed Linsey out of the supermarket.

"What do you want?"

"I…"

"You don't live around here. I've never seen you here before, and now that you come to my house, here you are again. Who sent you?"

"No one," Linsey blurted. "I was just passing."

"To where?"

Linsey knew she had been rumbled. The truth now was her only option.

"Patricia."

"How do you know my name? I never gave it to you."

Linsey looked down and put her hands in her jeans.

"It was on an envelope near your front door. One of crew read it."

"I knew it. All that you can trust me rubbish. You're all the same. Two-faced liars."

"Patricia, please. I'm sorry."

"Sorry! I should report this harassment."

"Please hear me out; if you want to report me, then do so."

"Pat!"

A young lad on a bike skidded up next to them.

"Mum said to come a get you. Ben has had a fall."

"What?"

"Down the stairs. He's alright, a bit quiet."

She looked at the young lad, then down at her work smock. She took her keys out of her pocket and thumbed a sign towards the shop.

"Bag," was all she said. She took a step towards the shop, then stopped.

"Shit."

"Go," said Linsey. "I'll go in and explain."

Two women looked at one another. One in hope, the other in desperation.

"I'll bring your bag if you want."

"Thanks, Ryan. Tell mum I'm coming."

She turned to Linsey.

"Ask for the duty manager, David. It's locker fourteen, and I still want that explanation."

She dropped the keys in Linsey's open palm and walked away through the cars.

Eddie walked over Tower Bridge and onto the south bank. The brighter side of the river was bathed in autumn sunshine.

The home to the London mayor, had a lambent glow. Tourists showed it their backs as they photographed the iconic bridge and tower. Ray had offered his son a small camera to take with him.

"It's a Contax, Son, easy to use and compact; you can keep it on your belt, see."

Eddie stood patiently while his father showed him how best to use it.

"Or just point and shoot. When you have a camera with you, when you go looking for that photo, you really look. You frame it in your mind, wonder if the light is right, and will it work against that bright backdrop? You examine the environment you're in with a measured eye all the time you're looking and keep it available, in your hand, ready for that candid shot, then…" Ray stopped and looked at his son. "Well, it's there if you want it."

Eddie thanked his father without committing. He'd always thought he had a measured eye, was good at taking in the surrounding environment. While he wouldn't mind having a go, he didn't want to meet Charlotte with a camera on his belt.

He was eager to see her, so he phoned and asked if she could meet earlier.

"Sure, where are you?"

He explained.

"Okay, well, I'm coming from Broadway."

"Broadway!"

"Yea, Fulham. So, how about you jump on at Tower Hill and we meet at Embankment?"

"You sure?"

"Definitely, can't wait."

The conversation had created so much nervous energy, he decided to walk to their rendezvous, but going up the stairs of the foot bridge adjacent to the rail crossing to get back to the north side of the Thames, he cursed himself. He felt hot and tired, and then, descending, he saw her waiting outside the entrance of the tube station. He was late.

"Sorry, Charlotte, have you been waiting long?" He kissed her on the cheek.

"Not as long as you, it would seem. Have you been admiring the view from up there?"

"No, I walked here."

"From Wapping," she said incredulously.

"Yea, nervous energy, needed burning."

She smiled her killer smile and added the lightest frown. His shyness revealed the boy inside the man; she liked it.

"Thirsty?"

"I could drink that dry." He pointed to the brackish river.

"Come on, I'll buy you a bottle of water, then cocktails."

"Where?"

"Simpsons."

Linsey was let in by the neighbour's babysitter.

"Come in, love, she's in there with Ben. He's alright, scared him a bit."

"You work with Pat, 'ere, ah give me those. I'm Brenda."

Linsey handed the bag and fleece to Brenda, then walked softly to the living room door as if approaching intensive care.

Patricia sat facing away from the door on the edge of the sofa, stroking Ben's hair. He lay on his side watching the telly.

Linsey tapped on the architrave.

Patricia didn't turn. She was expecting the unwanted guest.

"Yea."

"I brought your stuff."

"Thanks."

"Can I come in?"

"Well, you're here now."

Linsey stood next to mum and looked down at the patient. Both ignored her.

"Did he bang his head?"

"Bren saw him do it, said no."

"Cup of tea you two?" Bren asked.

Ben brushed the attentive hand away. She stood.

"I'll do it, Bren. You get going, and thanks again."

Linsey was back in the kitchen, but this time, as a civilian. The air of existential authority was gone now as she was out of uniform.

Patricia placed two mugs of tea on the table and motioned for Linsey to sit. "That's for doing me a favour. While you drink it, you tell me why you're here and when it's gone, so are you."

Linsey collected her thoughts.

"I ain't been in the fire service long, but I love it. I love helping the community, and we are, by and large, appreciated, even liked. People are pleased to see us, grateful."

Patricia sighed.

"I don't want people to be grateful, Patricia; sorry, I was just saying. Then, I came into your home and for the first time, there was someone who not only didn't want us here…"

Linsey looked around the sparse, clean kitchen.

"But seemed…"

She hesitated.

"Scared; you looked scared of us, Patricia, and it has worried me since. I know what I done today was stupid, but I just wanted a chance to talk to you. Unofficial like."

Patricia got up and put her cup in her new bowl. She turned and leant back on the sink. The light from the window behind her cast her in silhouette.

"So, you want me to free you of any feeling of guilt, eh, because you scared me, got it wrong with your overbearing presence. So, well done, great job, what would we do without you? Finished your tea?"

Linsey resigned herself to Pat's animus. She took out a small notebook and withdrew the slim pencil from its spine.

"My name is Linsey Rivers. This is the telephone number of Langden Fire Station. It's ex-directory. Ask for ADO Siddall, he is the officer in charge of the station. You can report my behaviour to him." She tore out the page and left it on the table.

Linsey stood.

"Once again, I'm sorry. Can I just say before I go that if Ben complains of a headache, take him to A&E and don't let him fall asleep." Patricia Arnold nodded.

"One more thing."

"What now?"

"Can I use your loo? My request in the shop was genuine, I'm busting."

"Door in front of you, top of the stairs."

Linsey climbed the stairs, hoping not to see a trip hazard. Pointing it out to Pat would increase her ire to an attack level. The carpet was new-looking and in good order. Ben must have been unlucky.

In the hall, Patricia opened the front door. Ben could be heard laughing at the telly. Linsey noticed how far from the front door her table was. Two paces if that. She could forgive the slight transgression by the crew, but would be left wondering what the serious offence was that the fire service had committed.

The day was going well. Charlotte met Eddie with an enthusiasm normally kept for old and trusted friends. Since their initial meeting, she had decided to give Eddie the benefit of the doubt. He seemed like a nice guy. Two drinks diluted his shyness and his self-deprecating conversation was amusing and in sharp contrast to men she knew at work. Her private life had been devoid of male company since her failed marriage. She liked his focus. Hated it when men gazed around the room while she spoke; he never.

She recalled him standing in front of the Turner. In the cocktail lounge, he removed his black bomber jacket and folded it carefully onto the empty chair next to him revealing the tartan interior. The slim fit white shirt with button down collar covered but didn't hide his broad shoulders and flat stomach. He wore no jewellery apart from a rather small and old-looking watch in contrast to the gaudy chunks of metal preferred generally by men.

He noticed her looking at it.

"My father gave it to me recently."

"It's nice. Is it very old?"

"Dad said at least sixty years. My grandfather's, a…"

Eddie looked past her for the first time as he recalled his father's description. "Rose gold cushion watch, Bravington Renown. Keeps perfect time."

"Really? You were late."

He shrugged and smiled.

"Actually, you were early. I pride myself on my punctuality."

"Well, we have something in common."

"Oh, we have so much in common."

"Such as?" She sipped her drink.

Eddie had finished his drink. He agitated the ice with the twizzle stick.

"Paintings."

As he said it, he knew he was going to lose this round of verbal sparring.

"Of course. What's your favourite period?"

"I like all periods but my favourite, my absolute favourite."

He was desperately trying to recall the term he had used in Clarence's office while simultaneously enjoying the glee on Charlotte's face. He needed to say something stupid. Humour was the bridge to safer ground from the corner he had painted himself into.

"My absolute favourite, would you like another drink?"

She shook her head, barely containing a smile.

"Well, it's got to be Extract Depressionists."

Her laugh scrunched up her nose, which was followed by the lightest snort. "Oops." Charlotte covered her mouth and nose with a flat, delicate hand. Eddie pushed home his advantage.

"Yes, early Extract Depressionists."

His joke, now without surprise, had lost its punch. Charlotte recovered her composure.

"Why were you there that day?"

Eddie shrugged as he pushed his glass away.

"At a loose end, I suppose."

Then another punchline started to gestate in his mind.

"I was looking for something."

"What was that, Ed?"

"Beauty, yea, I had read the article sitting at my father's table that morning, and I went in search of beauty."

"And did you find it?"

"In spades."

Some of the Italian restaurants in Soho date back to the 1950s when there was a large Italian community living in the heart of London. Charlotte knew a good one in Frith Street.

After the second drink, she had asked Eddie if he minded walking a little more.

"Another one of those and you'll be carrying me."

"Sure, I'm raring to go."

Covent Garden thrummed with life from the energetic street artists stringing out their acts as long as possible to living statues that only moved when paid. Large groups of one sex or the other stood outside pubs and bars, all talking simultaneously. Everyone ignored the young lad in his sleeping bag, sitting in a doorway. A middle-aged man displaying every sign of a hard life shouted 'Big Issue'. Eddie and Charlotte navigated their path to Soho, enjoying the atmosphere. She had slipped her hand in his when leaving the cocktail lounge, then once over Strand, she moved it up to the crook of his arm, which he bent to oblige her. Her other hand rested on his bicep.

He felt her squeeze it slightly.

Back in Wapping, Ray had walked the half mile or so to the Town of Ramsgate for a swift half. He would then return home and warm his stew. He sat at a polished wooden table, nursing his arm that kept him company with a dull ache.

He had struggled since moving back up the smoke. He thought about the house back in Stanford. How, over the years, he had toiled to make it a pleasant place to be, followed Eve around cleaning up after her and her outrageous ideas, subduing her eclectic style. He dug and hoed the garden, planted shrubs, mowed the lawn, then, after her sudden death, had the patio laid that she had always wanted. All this, all those years, then on the day he left for London, he could have been a dispassionate businessman eager to vacate an overnight hotel room, keen to move on. He hoped he had not made a mistake.

He had never been a gregarious man. Companionship with one other person was enough. Since Phylis had died some three years ago, his life had walked a lonely path. His home in Stanford with Eve was lively. It wouldn't be anything else with Eve, the epitome of gregariousness, but they had long decided to go their own ways. They shared a mutual respect, perhaps a love that comes with living together for so many years, but intimacy was a fruit long withered on the vine. Then, there was Eddie, the son he always blamed for trapping him in a loveless marriage. He worried that his reserved demeanour had leached into his son's character and tainted his life.

He had been a fool.

The one silver lining to all this was that since his reconciliation with his son, Eddie had appeared happier and more at ease with him.

As he finished his beer, his attention was drawn to a couple at the next table. The man had a resigned expression while he listened to what he was being told.

"You can't play football tomorrow, there's too much to do. I want this dinner to go without a hitch. You will have to go shopping for…" Ray zoned out of the diatribe.

He thought about another drink; he thought about sitting there all night and getting smashed. He decided one was enough. He would stroll home and maybe ask Meena if she would like to share his stew, maybe.

Ray stood and took his glass to the bar. On his way out, he passed the couple, smiled at the man, and stepped out the door.

"Tell me about your job," asked Eddie after he had let Charlotte decide which side of the small deuce she wanted to sit on. He had his back to the door.

They had ordered and were enjoying another drink. He had an Italian lager, she a white wine spritzer.

"On second thoughts, that can wait. Tell me about you, family, everything."

"Everything! On a first date," she said playfully.

"Well, let's make it our second."

"Our first being?"

"In the crypt at St Martin's."

"Ok, well, seeing as we are an established couple with history, I assume it's time I spilt the beans."

"I don't even know how old you are."

"Nor I you."

"That's important for an established couple."

"I remember as a child asking my father the same question. We love to tease children, don't you think? Straightforward answers to one's offspring appear to be an anathema. 'As old as my tongue, darling, and slightly older than my teeth', he would repeat whenever I asked."

"Did it frustrate you?"

"Then probably, now just remembrance of things past."

Charlotte was enjoying her drink.

Eddie loved her use of language.

"Have you ever seen this the other way around?"

"Never been here before."

She giggled. "The drinks. Have you ever been aware of the man ordering a spritzer and the woman a beer?"

"Well, I've never been a big drinker, but my last girlfriend only drank Stout and Mild."

As the food was served, Charlotte knew she had made the right choice. The bruschetta, well, that always was a dead cert.

Sean Stolly arrived for his first night shift on the Red at Langden. He had introduced himself to the guvnor, then to Ken.

"Hallo, mate, how's tricks?"

"Hallo, Ken. Well, I'm pleased to see you're still in the kitchen. They say your reputation precedes you in this job, and your reputation as a good mess manager certainly does that."

"Crawler, full messing?"

"Of course."

"That's what I like to hear."

He then got the keys to his locker and threw his bedding on one of the two cots in the leading firefighter's room. The room he would be sharing with the other leading hand, Chris Everett, who happened to join him while Sean placed his toiletries on the top shelf of his locker.

"Hallo, Sean, welcome to Red Watch. Got everything?"

"Yea, thanks. It's Alec, right?"

"Yea, that's right."

Chris was pleased Sean had taken the bed vacated by John Mullins, so they didn't start out with any awkwardness.

"Everyone calls me Chris, though."

"Why's that?"

Chris felt his scalp tingle. He hated these conversations.

"Well, I'll give you three guesses."

Sean's mouth turned down in an ignorant grimace. He added a light shake of the head.

"Everett, Chris Evert, tennis player. Some wag thought it funny, and it has stuck."

"I thought Kenny might be more appropriate."

Chris knew the famous Kenny Everett, who had been a TV and radio star and was a gay man.

Was Sean referring to the same spelling of his and Kenny's name or the fact that he, too, was gay? He ran his hand over his head and decided to let it slide. "Yeah, guess so, but I'm stuck with Chris now. What about you, a different handle than Sean?"

Sean Stolly closed and locked the metal cabinet and clipped the keys to a chain that extended from his belt loop into his pocket.

"Been known as the Nazi."

"Ok, the reason being?"

"I'll give you one guess."

Chris knew the answer but preferred to feign ignorance.

"Nah, you got me there."

"My initials. Arthur said I'm in charge of the water tender."

"Yea, Eddie's off both nights."

"So, I get the busy bus, first night here. Great."

With that, he walked out of the room.

"Yea, great," murmured Chris to himself.

The Italian waiter was experienced in his craft. He wanted to remove the remains of the first course without interrupting the couple, whose eyes were feasting on one another. He would give them a few more minutes and attend to the man and woman staring vacantly about the restaurant, their conversation as empty as their plates.

Charlotte relaxed back in her chair. The food had a sobering effect. She collected her thoughts, then started.

"I come from Bagshot in Surrey; well, near it. My father is a judge, mummy is a housewife, though we must not refer to her as that, and I have a sister, two years younger, who lives in the States, married to an airline pilot whom she met while teaching near Mildenhall in Suffolk."

"May I?" The waiter asked. Their time up on the first course.

Eddie's thoughts confirmed his earlier appraisal. He was definitely punching. "Now, it's your turn. Excuse me…" She caught the waiter's attention before he escaped to the kitchen. "May we have some water, please?"

"Certainly, Madam. Tap?"

"Perrier."

"Of course."

Eddie considered a humorous response, then thought better of it. Charlotte may well intuit evasion of the truth as a sinister mask.

"I grew up on a council estate in Stanford le Hope. My parents came from East London. My father worked in factories; my mother for a solicitor. My mother was killed last year in a road traffic collision. Since then, my dad moved back up here. I'm an only child."

Two waiters arrived, one with the bottle of water, the other with the main courses. Noise from the kitchen escaped as more dishes were brought to hungry customers. The front door was held open for people leaving. A woman near the door looked around and shuddered. The infinitesimal change in temperature drifted over the room, wrapping itself around the diners' subconsciousness.

The first veil of Charlotte and Eddie's mystique had slipped away.

The water fizzed and the ice cracked as their main courses were placed in front of them.

"Parmesan?"

They both gave a subdued shake of the head.

"Buon appetite," said the waiter, leaving them to their repast.

Sean Stolly and Linsey sat in the cab outside Sainsbury's. Ken needed a few things for the evening meal; Billy Butler was helping him.

"So, you were a bus driver?"

"That's right, Sean, vans then buses," said Linsey, fiddling with her seat adjustment.

"What's the matter? Trouble reaching the pedals?"

Linsey forced a laugh. "Yea."

"Have you driven to a shout yet?"

"No, I'm still just doing ordinary runs, getting used to the lorries."

"I remember finishing my driving course. First day back and the guvnor said 'You're driving the rescue pump'."

"Wow, in at the deep end." Linsey tried to sound impressed.

"Yea, it was different back then. Men were men and sheep were scared, heh heh. How do you get on with the rest of the watch?"

"Fine, I think I landed on my feet with this lot."

"Well, if you get any problems, let me know."

"What do you mean?"

"You know." He eyed her up and down. "Anyone starts sniffing around."

"No, no, they are a great bunch," she replied, appalled by the thought. "I'm sure Ken even thinks he's my dad."

"Whatever."

Sean opened his window and spat onto the road before bestowing his opinion of the watch upon her.

"Yea, great bunch, the firefighters. Arthur is sound as a pound. Eddie…" He shrugged. "He's alright, can be a bit pompous and then Chris. Well, at least you won't get any problems from Chris." He lisped the name. "No, you're right, he's a good man."

Her first impressions of Sean Stolly sitting around the mess table earlier had now changed considerably. There, he had laughed and joked with the ones he knew, shook hands with the others, including her, and said he was pleased to be here. He now exuded an air of sullen vindictiveness.

"I'm the one who's got to watch out, eh?"

"Sorry."

"Sharing a room with him. If I drop my wallet, I'll have to kick it to the wall before bending to pick it up."

"That's a terrible thing to say."

"Alright, keep ya bra on."

The doors to the rear cab opened and Ken and Billy jumped in.

"Got everything?" Sean asked.

"Yes, thanks."

"I've been talking to Linsey about her driving and decided if we get a shout on the way back, she can take it unless it's persons reported." Linsey shot him a nervous glance.

"But…" He paused for comic effect. "She mustn't pull over at bus stops." The three men laughed as she fired the engine.

Eddie and Charlotte strolled down Villiers Street to Embankment tube station. Both didn't want the evening to end, but the circumstances, as Charlotte saw it, dictated that end it must. They were arguing, albeit politely, the way friends do over who pays and getting home.

After the restaurant where Charlotte insisted on splitting the bill, they walked to The Coach and Horses. Customers crowded the bar holding tens and twenties up as they endeavoured to flag down the bar staff. The smell of alcohol and tobacco was cloying. The linoleum floor was sticky with beer. A pianist was tickling the ivories. The wood-panelled bar back advertised Skoll Lager and Ind Coope. The gold lettering was illuminated by electric candelabra hanging on long cable flex from the high ceiling. Framed pictures of celebrities and cartoons adorned the walls. Laughter broke out in sporadic bursts of contagion.

"I love this place," she said to Eddie as he returned from the bar with their drinks. His elbows were close to his body in a practised style, preventing unwanted spillage.

"It's like going back in time."

"Not a time you remember surely," he said. He still didn't know her age.

"No, but one I can imagine. When the men went to the bar, thanks." She took her drink. "The women sat in the snug and never had to open their purses." She tasted her wine before continuing. Eddie could see she approved of his lucky choice.

"My father used to take us to a Swiss restaurant, long gone, he loved it; the alpine version of meat and two veg. He enjoyed explaining the menu and conversing with the staff. He speaks German."

"Did you enjoy it?" Eddie asked.

"Some dishes were as heavy as my mother's handbag, but yes, and it meant the four of us got together for a family meal, which was rare because of my father's workload. Anyway, it wasn't until my late teens that, on one of these occasions, I realised that there were two different menus. Could you guess in what way?"

Eddie pretended to think.

"No," he said.

"The menu offered to the woman had no prices on it. The financial privilege of the bill was the sole preserve of the man."

Charlotte was nudged from behind, and a trickle of wine ran over her fingers.

"Sorry, luv."

Eddie mouthed an alright to the man and suggested they move nearer the window.

"So, the paradox," she said, "is that it's nice to look back, but I'm glad we have moved on."

Now in Villiers Street, below the blue plaque of Rudyard Kipling, she insisted she get the tube to Fulham alone.

Eddie, while not wanting to appear patriarchal, genuinely wanted to see her safely home and pressed his concern upon her.

"Eddie, it's not that late. I've done this journey many times, and my walk from the Broadway to my house is not far. Besides, I've got the Glock in my bag."

"But..."

They had stopped walking. Charlotte stood on the pavement, Eddie in the gutter. She placed her hand on his chest and, before he could remonstrate further, kissed him with a lingering softness on his mouth. Her other hand caressed the back of his neck.

Eddie took his hands out of his bomber and was about to embrace her when she pulled back.

The taste of her lips strengthened his resolve.

She anticipated this and, with modest firmness, explained, "Eddie, if I let you walk me to my door, I would drag you to the other side of London and, therefore, feel obliged to ask you in. I don't want that. Not tonight, not this time. Please?"

Eddie nodded.

"Just one thing."

"What's that?" She asked.

"Could we try that kiss again?"

Linsey lay in her cot in the dorm. She was trying to read but couldn't concentrate. She was still excited about driving to her first shout. They had just left the supermarket when the main scheme radio sparked into life with a priority message telling them to proceed to fire alarms actuating in a children's home on the other side of town.

She loved the way the two lines of traffic parted like a wave in front of her and then gave her right of way at junctions and roundabouts. The complete opposite of how other road users treat buses. People stopped to watch; she was the centre of attention in this exciting spectacle, flying down the road. Sean was an expert with the two tones and she never had to worry about using them herself. Her adrenaline flowed, increasing her acuity. They arrived first. Sean, Ken, and Billy disappeared into the home while she engaged the power takeoff and went to the rear of the appliance, ready to pump water if required. The rescue pump had pulled up immediately behind them. She could see Arthur in the front talking on a two-way radio, probably to Sean. Luke Dunstford strolled over to her.

"Ah, makes sense now."

"What?" Linsey replied, already on the defensive.

"We couldn't work out why you lot were going so slow. Thought the engine had packed up and you were coasting here."

Her elation popped like a needle in a balloon, but she wouldn't give Luke the pleasure of knowing it.

"Faster than you ever manage."

"Oh yea, it was so slow, there are flies stuck to the back. Look."

She glanced up involuntarily. "Ha, got ya," said Luke.

"Fuck off, Puke."

By this time, her crew were coming back. It was a false alarm.

Linsey went to get back behind the wheel when Sean stopped her.

"Let Billy take it now."

"Why, Sean?"

"Your adrenaline's up. Can have the opposite effect when driving normally. Until you're more experienced, don't want a prang, do we?"

She climbed into the rear cab and sat next to Ken.

"Well done," he said quietly.

She had played the journey over and over in her mind, getting faster every time, then wondering how she could have improved upon it.

Luke was a dick but she would have worried more if he'd complimented her. She tried to read. No, no good. She got up and went down to the gym.

Maybe some bench presses and sit-ups would help.

14

Charlotte woke early. Sunday was her favourite day. She would get up and make tea, then bring it back to bed and enjoy the hot malt flavour wash away the night while she read another chapter. First, though, she would languish under her goose down duvet, placed on her bed only yesterday with the coming winter in mind. She wanted the excitement of last night to keep her company a while longer. Insisting he didn't come back with her was a tough call. One-night stands are ok when that's all one wants but when desiring something more, rushing it had, in the past, been to her detriment. The one thing she had decided early last night was that she wanted more. She ran her hands up her thighs while remembering the taste of his lips, feeling just the tip of his tongue.

She hated another tongue invading her mouth with dominating force. He had stepped back, just a half pace, after the kiss, then exhaled, not wanting his beer and garlic breath to spoil their first intimate moment. Considerate or self-centred, confident or shy, he was hard to read. Right now, those traits could bide their time. She wanted to think about that taut frame, muscled arms, his cute arse, and as she did so, her right hand sought an intimacy to accompany her sensual reflections.

Eddie's hand flew away from his cock mimicking an electric shock when his father knocked and walked immediately into his bedroom with a mug of tea. "There ya go, Son. Hope that's how you like it. Perhaps, you'll do the breakfast. I'd like it before lunch."

It was seven-thirty. Eddie sat up in bed.

"Thanks, Dad, I'll be right with ya."

Ray looked back from the doorway. "Good, and wash your hands first." Before Eddie could counter Ray's remark, he was gone.

He touched the mug and decided to let it cool. He was getting to know his father more. The cold, elusive man of his childhood had a sense of humour. A sunnier disposition was gradually emerging. Was it too late? No. Better late than never.

It was too late for thoughts of Charlotte, though. His reverie, so cruelly interrupted, would have to wait. The spell was broken, but his mind had other ideas. He wanted her, had wanted her from that first meeting. The physical attraction was consuming him in moments at a glance. Of course, he had stared into her chocolate brown eyes, admired her slender, dimpled chin, but the rest, well, at a glance. He had noticed her athletic legs. Glancing at them at every opportunity, they flicked out from the knee, set wide on broad hips, and finished with slender ankles. He was a leg man, and they looked beautiful. It wasn't enough, he wanted to see her properly.

To stare at her as she lay naked on a bed, to photograph with his mind's eye every soft undulation. To watch how she reacted to his caress. He wanted to turn her on with his longing for her, admire her as she lay undisguised before him.

He picked up his phone, as early as it was, but he couldn't wait.

"Good morning," she said.

She sounded dreamy, he hoped he hadn't woken her.

"How do you like your eggs?"

There was that little giggle again.

"Over easy," she replied. "You?"

"Coddled."

"Really? Do you coddle your eggs regularly?"

She arched her back, enjoying the luxury of her bed and the silly conversation.

"Of course. In fact, I'm going to coddle a couple now for my father."

"Oh, he likes them too?"

"Yep, runs in the family."

A slight pause told Eddie to move on.

"Thanks for last night," he said. "I really enjoyed myself."

"All of it?"

"Yes, all of it."

"No one part in particular?"

She had rolled onto her stomach. Leaning on her elbow, she held the phone to her ear, her other hand cupping her breast.

"Well, you insisting on going Dutch, result, and the look on your face when that bloke knocked into you spilling your drink, that was funny, and how after two cocktails you had to hold on to me, hilarious."

He lay back on the bed. Charlotte remained silent.

"When you laughed at my stupid jokes. The fact that you got them was novel, and the way you described your family or spoke about anything, really. The way you phrase a sentence, your voice. The way you held my arm wasn't hilarious. It was—well, I don't want to say nice, it's such a sickly word—but the way you held my arm was nice." He could hear her breathing.

"The delicate way you touch your mouth with the napkin before speaking. The way you bite your bottom lip when considering your reply. I loved watching you think. The sexy way you walk. The way you held the back of my neck when we kissed, so tender, and the kiss, kisses so gentle and…"

"And what?"

"Hypnotic."

White noise fizzed between the two mobile phones. Eddie hoped he hadn't gone too far. He felt overexposed.

"Come over this afternoon," she said, then hung up.

The Red were having breakfast. They were grumpy, having had a night of interruptions. Three more times they had returned to the children's home. The manager explained that they had a new intake of kids who were particularly disruptive and setting off the alarms. Ken suggested chaining them to their beds, which brought a nervous titter from the man in charge. Then, once, to a small factory unit where again it was fire alarms and, this time, they had to wait for a key holder; there being no sign of fire, so no desperate need to gain entry by smashing down the front door.

"We should smash down the front door every time their alarm goes off. Then they would make sure it worked properly."

"Yes, Puke, good way to serve the community."

"It's alright for you. You ain't got kids. I'll go home in the morning, and it will be daddy do this and daddy do that."

"Regret having them?" Billy Butler asked.

"Fuck off, Bill, it's alright for you with only your cock to keep." Billy looked at Linsey.

"I'll probably go home, lie on the couch with the papers and a brew, and if I nod off, then lovely. What about you, Lins?"

"Some of the same, I think. Maybe in the garden if it's warm enough in our little sun trap. I love a lazy Sunday."

Luke knew not to take the bait and strolled over to the car that had just pulled up in front of the factory.

The water tender went out one more time to a woman locked out. She had arrived home from a night out in Chelmsford and realised her keys were in the first-floor flat.

"You alright, sweetheart?" Ken asked. "Good night out?"

"Yea, sorry, ain't got me keys."

Billy was looking up.

"That fan light is open, Sean." He pointed to the side window. "Could put the triple ex up to it. I reckon I could get in."

Sean was about to agree to the plan when the young woman said, "Ooh no, not that one."

"Why not?" Sean asked.

"You'll wake my old man."

Billy and Linsey already had the ladder off the appliance.

"Put it back on," said Sean. "Ring the bell, Ken, and get her old man up."

"Can you believe the fucking audacity of these sorts?" Sean said in the cab as they were about to drive away. "Fucking women. Fucking time wasting tarts too stupid to remember their keys."

"She was drunk," said Ken.

"She was a cunt," said Sean.

"Want to drive back, Lins?" Billy asked.

"No, you're ok," she replied.

Right then, Linsey preferred the rear cab.

They were eating toast, eggs, and bacon in weary silence when Arthur came into the mess.

"I put yours in the warmer, Guv," said Ken.

"Cheers, Ken. Listen up, everyone. I've been on the blower with John. He wants his retirement drink next Friday. All welcome, bring the wives if you've got one. Billy, you can come with me."

They tried a laugh, but their hearts weren't in it.

"Ok," said Arthur, sighing. "Well, I hope you can all make it."

"Where's he 'avin it, Guv?" Perry asked.

"Good point, Perry. Cloud Nein, you know it down by the station."

"Pricey," said Jim.

"Oh, I forgot to mention it. Free bar, he's putting a wad up front."

"I've always liked Cloud Nein," said Ken, wiping his bread around his plate.

In the kitchen in Wapping, Ray was supervising his son's cleaning. He insisted Eddie wear the yellow rubber gloves while washing up. It allowed you to have really hot water in the bowl.

"How was your night, Son?"

"I had a really…" *Here's that word again*, thought Eddie. "Nice night." He didn't want to overegg it. He felt shy in front of his old man and did not want to alert Ray to his enthusiasm.

"Nice, eh? Not that one, that's for your hands, the other cloth is dishes."

"Yea, nice, and you?"

"Well, I had a really nice night. Got smashed in the pub, brought a load of complete strangers back, and partied till late."

"There's a part of me that wants to believe that, Dad."

"Yea, me too. I did pop out for one. Have you ever tried getting money out of your wallet one-handed? Nightmare. Anyway, came home, gave Meena a knock, and asked if she'd like to share my stew."

"And?"

"She declined; said she doesn't like English food."

"You should have said it's an Irish stew," said Eddie playfully while putting away the crockery.

"Well, that is the same as saying it's not an Indian dish, it's Pakistani."

"I'm sure there's a huge…"

"You know what I mean," said Ray, interrupting. "So, I ate half and froze the rest."

"Well, her loss is your gain."

Ray thought back to his evening alone, eating his dinner, and didn't quite see it like that.

"That dish doesn't go there, it goes down there," said Ray as his son put the last of the breakfast things away.

15

The North Sea was being dragged out of London like a drunk from a barroom brawl. 'You know I will return', it said, 'and when the sun, earth and moon are aligned, when the atmosphere is low in pressure, I will overwhelm your ignorant walls, your desperate defences, and the land will be mine'. The city watched stupefied behind its stony facades as the strung-out sea receded to other shores, revealing the dark eel of the Thames. Safe for now, the capital's concerned refrain.

The river from source to sea runs past countless lives like a long take in a Scorsese film. It cups Fulham in a shallow u-bend. On the west side, rowers work hard against its flow; swans ready their young for their first winter. Here, Charlotte is humming a song. She has tidied up, there is food and wine in the fridge. She sits on the edge of her bath, a vanity mirror is placed precariously next to the sink taps. She plucks her eyebrows. She could have left this job another day, but decided to busy herself with this mundane yet important task that would add to her confidence when this man holds her in his arms.

From there, the dark eel glides along the central tideway, supporting pleasure boats full of tourists and barges bursting with the city's detritus destined for Essex landfill. Ever onwards, the river assumes the path of least resistance east to Wapping. Here, Eddie is wiping the shaving mirror. Steam from the sink had obscured his reflection. Eddie felt from the back of his jaw around his chin and over his cheek. Smooth as a baby's bum, he thought. He did not like the style of stubble beard. A full beard required attention and grooming; stubble, well, that was plain laziness. He wanted Charlotte to see he cared.

Ray was in the living room watching actors pretending to be tough guys. His wrist throbbed, but he couldn't be bothered to get up and take his painkillers. Eddie could get a glass of water for himself. He liked being looked after by his son. Maybe he will come more often, he thought, if this relationship with Charlotte flourishes.

From Wapping, the dark eel has to get a wriggle on and chase the receding tide through the Thames barrier, all the way to the estuary. Now, the traffic is getting serious. Large cargoes from everywhere, passenger liners and ferry boats, seals and the occasional porpoise live and work in this infamous thoroughfare. To the mouth it glides, the wide watery expanse that is at once the dolorous end and the luminescent beginning.

Here, on the north bank, Linsey is in a contemplative mood. The night shift was a mixed bag. She had driven to her first shout and felt confident that she performed well. On the other hand, the new officer unsettled her. Sean knew what he was doing and she was sure to learn from him; it was how he went about it that was problematic. Like he said, he was old school, said it like it is. His world was tough and male-dominated, where, she guessed, you had to fight your corner. Perhaps that will have to be her attitude. That was the phrase the female police officer had used—what was her name? Chloe, yea—fight your corner. Yep, she was sure she could do that; she would have to.

16

Eddie stood outside the two up two two-down in Maxwell Street. It had been an easy journey across town on the District Line. How he loved that name. Full of Victorian functionality. The walk from the tube didn't take long, so he still felt fresh from his shower, unlike yesterday's riverside hike. He rang the bell and as he waited, he realised he had come empty-handed. No flowers, no wine, nothing; what an idiot. He remembered the shops he passed on his way from the station and turned on his heel, thinking if she hadn't heard the chime, he would be able to nip back a get something, anything.

Charlotte opened the door.

"Changed your mind?"

"Hiya. No, I was…"

Eddie turned to face her, dropped his shoulders, and bared his open palms. "Forgot the wine."

Charlotte placed one foot on her outside doormat and pointed.

"There is a lovely wine shop on the Broadway. I'd say a mile from here, but it will definitely be open."

"Right, won't be long."

"Come in, silly. I'm joking, got plenty."

She closed the front door and kissed him long enough to mean more than hallo. He kissed her back. The tips of their tongues released a desire that would have to be sated.

Charlotte pulled him close and nibbled his ear. Eddie was trying to remove his jacket and shuck off his shoes.

"No small talk," she whispered.

"No."

"No house tour." She kissed his neck.

"No."

"No drinks." She kissed his mouth, then his chin.

"No."

"Nothing."

"Everything."

"Everything."

Linsey was woken by her phone. In the seconds before she collected her thoughts, she was unaware of her location and devoid of any thought.

"Linsey, Linsey darling, it's mum."

"Hi, Mum."

"You alright, luv? You sound dopey."

"You woke me, Mum, fell asleep on the sofa."

"Hungover?"

"No, busy night."

"Anyway, if you're free, pop over for dinner. The boys are here. Your father is roasting a piece of topside that would feed a pride of lions. So, come and help us out, darling."

"Short notice, Mum."

"Well, I never know when you are at work or not with that silly shift of yours."

"Not that hard, Mum."

"Your dad's the same."

"I gave you my rota card that tells you when I'm at work for the whole year."

"I know, Lins, but it's all those other colours. What are you doing then?"

"They are the other watches, Mum."

"Exactly, totally confusing. I wonder if they would eat it cooked or want it raw."

"What, Mum?"

"The lions I wonder if lions…"

"I'll see you in an hour, Mum, bye."

Nancy, Michelle, and Linsey sat on the large L-shaped settee. Bradley sat on the floor close to his mother's legs. He was playing with an electronic game.

It annoyed Nancy when he kept knocking her leg with his elbow.

"Bradley! For god's sake."

"What you playing, Bradley? Wanna show me?" Linsey asked.

Bradley shook his head without answering.

Michelle was feeding her daughter.

"At work last night, Lins, how was it?" She asked, rubbing the baby's back.

"Oh, in and out like a fiddler's elbow." She loved Ken's terminology. "But nothing to shout about. New bloke started. When I say new, I mean he transferred in. Leading hand."

Raised voices came from the kitchen. Nancy looked around to see, then smoothed her dress.

"I take it you mean an officer," said Michelle.

"Ooh, does he share your bedroom, Lins?" Nancy asked keen for anything salacious.

"No, thank god."

"Why would you be afraid of succumbing to his charms? Bradley! Move away."

"Charms, I don't think he has any."

"Why?" Michelle asked.

Linsey thought about sidestepping the subject, but decided she could do with some feminine intuition.

"Well, it's been one night, ok. I could be wrong about him, but first impressions count, right?"

Her sisters-in-law nodded, not wanting to delay the reveal.

Linsey continued.

"His attitude towards women, from what I heard last night, is appalling."

"How?" Michelle asked.

"His language when talking about a female member of the public was gross. He was so dismissive and vile about her situation. Told me to keep my bra on when I challenged him on something he said earlier in the evening."

"What was the situation?" Michelle asked.

"Middle of the night, women locked out, but her husband was asleep inside, and she wanted us to help her get in."

"Duh, ring the doorbell."

"Yea, Nancy, but her bloke might be violent, she might have been scared. She might have wanted a bit of support."

"Is that your job, Lins, really?"

Linsey ignored Nancy's comments.

"To him, she was a…" Linsey looked at Bradley. "The C word, an effing time waster."

Michelle could see the concern on Linsey's face; she frowned.

"So, he is sexist," said Nancy, looking at her phone.

"Misogynist," said Michelle.

"Is there a difference?" Nancy asked.

"Most men have sexist attitudes even when they argue that they haven't. But misogyny is different, it's deeper. It's hatred."

Michelle looked at her daughter, sound asleep in her lap.

"Well, you can't say that for sure, Miche, after one night. He might just be a rufty-tufty fireman who's not used to working with our Lins here and speaks his mind."

"We have a gay firefighter on the watch, and his attitude towards him is no better."

"A gay firefighter!" Nancy exclaimed. "I bet he's definitely not allowed in the bedroom at night."

"Nancy, there are times when I despair of you."

"Oh, come on, Miche, I'm joking. I've worked, been around men, lots of them."

I bet you have, thought Linsey.

"I worked with a gay bloke once. Arsehole, wouldn't trust him as far as I could throw him and the blokes, well, you just have to handle them. You know you're going to hear things, risque things, but we can be like that too; bit of flirting never done no harm."

"Really!"

"Yes, Michelle, really. All this women's lib stuff. Stuff it, I say. I like having the door held open for me. I like the man paying and if I hear 'nice arse', well, quite frankly, it makes my day."

Linsey looked at Bradley. He seemed lost in his game.

Michelle put a hand on Linsey's wrist.

"Watch him, Linsey."

"You lot look deep in conversation," said Ange; she had wandered over from the kitchen, glass in hand.

"Come on, tell."

Nancy and Michelle both looked at Linsey.

Linsey, not wanting to go over it, tried to keep it light.

"Just talking about men, Mum. Where do you stand regarding women's lib?"

"Well…"

Angela took a sip of wine while she considered her response. She wanted to bring all her years of experience to bear for the benefit of her girls.

"Your dad has always called me his queen, likewise, I've always called him my king, but…"

She pointed to all three with her hand that held the glass.

"As we all know, once a king, always a king, but once a knight, that's enough."

"What's amused that lot?" Howard asked, responding to the laughter from the living room as he watched his father open the oven.

"Well, if it's your mother, it's probably smut," said his dad as he basted the roast potatoes with hot beef lard.

17

Charlotte and Eddie lay in each other's arms. They had made love twice. The first time was intensely passionate and quick. The second time was intensely passionate and slow. Her left leg lay across his stomach and her head on his shoulder. Eddie noticed the room for the first time as he lay there enjoying the feel of her naked body against his. There were clothes everywhere. On the chair near her dressing table, squeezed onto a hanging rail in an alcove by the chimney breast, and trying to escape from the wardrobe where they wouldn't allow the door to shut completely. He caressed her knee, then down to her ankle. Her skin was smooth and tanned from the long, hot summer.

Charlotte took hold of his hand as it traversed upwards to her thighs. Her thumb pushed into his palm, her fingers interlaced with his. She looked at the two hands in one embrace, his slightly larger.

"I like your hands."

"Really!"

Eddie was enjoying her kneading. He had never before appreciated the sensual intimacy it induced.

"Hmm, strong and firm. My…" She stopped mid-sentence.

Eddie looked her in the eye. "It's ok, you can say."

"No, sorry, I've known you five minutes and I start to talk about someone else."

"None of my ex-girlfriends massaged my hand like that. There, I've spoken of all mine in one go. Beat that."

He kissed her and ran his other hand from her shoulder down her back. Charlotte pushed her vulva against his leg and lowered hers to feel his crotch against her inner thigh.

"Ok, I'll do one better than girlfriends. My ex-husband had soft, pudgy hands, never liked them."

"That's all."

"Yes, he had a good physique; thick set, broad-shouldered, but his hands, no."

"Ok, you win."

She let go of his hand and then started to caress his nipple with her middle finger. He covered her shoulder from the chill autumn air in her unheated bedroom. "Can I ask why he's an ex-husband?"

He noticed her frown.

"It is our third date and we are lying naked in each other's arms." Charlotte stopped pushing against him with her hips. Eddie felt her withdrawal and wished he had curtailed his curiosity.

Her fingers maintained the caress of his chest. She ran them through the even spread of hair, noticing one or two grey strands. The last year had been really difficult for her. A somnambulant crawl through twelve months of misery from which she had just awoke. Could this conversation resurrect the nightmare? There was only one way to find out.

He was about to apologise when she started to speak. Her voice was quiet, any inflexion muted and monotone.

"I married when I was thirty. He was a year older. We were the perfect couple, everyone said so. He had or has an ebullient personality, plenty of friends who became my friends. Cricket in the summer, which the wives enjoyed socially. Squash in the winter, but it never stopped the ladies getting together for drinks. Good job in the city, and we were in love. He had plans, I loved his plans, so many. This house for a few years, then as his promotions at work came along, which everyone said would, a bigger house further out, Windsor maybe. That house, which he would describe to me, sounded wonderful, and it would have to be big because of all the children."

"He came from a family of four, two boys and two girls, and that's what he wanted because every sibling has a brother and sister, perfect. I'd say 'Hang on, four, don't forget it's me who's carrying them, let's start with two and see how we go'. He would laugh and say two sets of twins, easy. We never tried for the first year; this place took up most of our time, but once we felt established here, I stopped taking the pill."

Although Eddie's arm started to feel numb, he wouldn't break her train of thought by asking to move.

"Pressure builds slowly like a dissenting voice in a troubled throng. It can only be ignored for so long. We tried to keep things light at the same time being inventive and practical, and well-read on the subject. Murmurings began. When are you starting a family, friends would ask; my mother was told off by father for prying. Then his sisters both became pregnant. I noticed the sadness in his eyes once as he watched his brother-in-law put his arms around his sister from behind and cup his unborn child in his arms. Then, the unavoidable question. I asked him over dinner if we should have tests, just to discount any condition, help us relax, and know it was just a matter of time."

"He never answered, just carried on with his dinner. Two weeks later, he came home and placed some paperwork in front of me. It said two hundred million per millilitre. 'What does this mean?' I asked stupidly. I'd been reading the books. 'It means it is a high sperm count', he said, 'your turn'. So, it was me, infertile."

"Charlotte, you don't have to tell me."

"Please." She stopped him. "It's time I did speak about it."

"Do you want a glass of wine?"

"Never thought you'd ask," he replied, wearing his friendliest smile.

They threw on their clothes and went downstairs to a warm lounge. While Charlotte made a noise in the kitchen, Eddie sat at the table in the living room and took in the disorder that surrounded him. All surfaces were occupied with figurines and plants. A small CD player had six CDs on top of it. A clock was partially obscured by a lava lamp. The low and old-looking leather settee was covered with a colourful throw and more cushions than necessary. Paintings and prints festooned the walls. The window at the front of the house was half-shuttered, negating the need for net curtains.

Charlotte placed food on the table and asked Eddie to open the wine. "Bread and cheese, ok?" She asked, sitting down.

"Excellent." Eddie was starving.

"Help yourself, please."

The wine glugged into the glasses.

Eddie felt he needed to say something innocuous, compliment her home or ask about the art, but decided to see if she wanted to continue.

She did.

"Have you ever watched a sci-fi film? Do you like films?"

"Love 'em."

"When the main protagonist wants to cross into another time zone or parallel universe and is stopped by an invisible force field. An unseeable but impenetrable wall."

He nodded, his mouth full of bread.

"That's what happened to us, an inconspicuous barrier. No one could see it; only he and I could feel it. Next, the inevitable. I knew he was having an affair. What wife doesn't? I suggested adoption, he looked at me with utter disdain."

"Then, he told me he was leaving me for her, she was pregnant. I could have the house, goodbye. Gone that same day." Charlotte raised the wine glass to her lips and drank deeply.

Eddie topped her up.

"He went, and everyone went with him. His friends and their wives, his family, everyone."

Charlotte continued to drink quickly.

"Suddenly, no one was interested in this dried-up husk. It has taken me a year to get over it, the shock of him leaving."

"Are you sure you are?"

"Yea, I know I am, but this is the first time I've unloaded like this. Sorry, it had to be you."

"How long were you married?"

"Seven years. So, now you know how old I am."

"Do I?"

"Married at thirty for seven plus one. What is it the Americans say? You do the math."

"Ah, forty."

"You make me laugh." She paused before saying, "Sorry, Ed."

"Say sorry again, and I'm off. I'm honoured that you chose me to unburden yourself to. What does he do?"

"All men ask that question. It is so important to you. Does it confirm hierarchy? The male pecking order."

"Don't know, just couldn't think of anything profound."

Charlotte looked at Eddie with a wine-laden intensity. She reached across the table and covered his hand with hers.

"He insures military aircraft."

"High flyer."

"Oh no, pathetic," she said, leaning back on her chair.

"Sorry."

"Say sorry again, and I'm kicking you out."

Eddie let a long sibilant 's' escape between his tongue and teeth before saying 'ok'.

"Do you want to go back to bed?" Charlotte asked.

"Well, I've got to make sure my old man is ok tonight, so just a quick two or three hours."

"Idiot."

Eddie hoped that was the wine talking and felt quite sure from the alluring smile on Charlotte's face that he was right.

Four hours later, he stood by her front door, putting on his shoes and jacket.

"Well, it's been lovely meeting you. We really should do this again sometime."

"You're such an idiot."

Charlotte leant against the small cast-iron radiator. She was wearing a heavy towelling bathrobe.

"I'm free tomorrow, until Friday actually."

She shook her head. "Busy week. Next weekend, yes."

"Ok, but it's going to be a long week."

"For me too."

Eddie wanted to run back to the tube station; he felt like a juvenile high on elation. Idiot, yes, that's what he was, a happy idiot.

Charlotte placed the glasses and plates on a tray and took them through to her small kitchen. She squeezed the tray next to the kettle, toaster, and the jars of dried herbs before pouring the last of the wine into her glass. A slight ripple of unease spread through her body. It had taken a year of hard endeavour to regain her self-confidence, and now here she was, standing in her kitchen, shaking, having let her guard down and revealing all to literally the first man she'd met since the collapse of her life. *Oh, Eddie Hart, please don't play me for the idiot that I am.*

18

Eddie looked at the local paper on the low coffee table. It was partially covered by two or three girlie mags that spread across the table's sticky veneer. He wondered what sort of coffee mornings John had.

Eddie was getting to know John quite well. The Red had been to his flat on a number of occasions, which included a flooding when John let the bath overflow, a kitchen fire when John set fire to his tea towel, and now this.

The source of these incidents for John's troubled mind was the local rag. A reporter was tasked with phoning the station daily and asking if there were any incidents worth reporting. The officer taking the call would detail the shouts, tell of the service's quick response and immediate intervention or rescue that ultimately saved the day. The reporter would thank the officer and ask for a name, and would be given one that belonged to a member from another watch. Most incidents made a few column inches on an inside page. John was an avid reader of the paper, taking in every detail of the shouts attended by Langden Fire.

So it transpired that when he read of a flooding, lo and behold, he had one. His kitchen fire followed soon after the one on page two, and when the bomb scare in the town centre made the front page, it was only a matter of time before this lonely, troubled soul discovered such a device in his home.

"It's under the table," said John, smoking nervously. He stood behind Eddie for protection.

"Ok, John, please wait outside while we deal with it."

Billy led him out.

Adam casually inspected the room.

"I'll look for secondary devices," he said to Eddie.

Eddie looked at the box of Maltesers under the table and kicked it out.

One day, a box of Maltesers will blow my foot off, he mused.

Eddie opened the box. He showed it to Adam.

"There's one left, want it?"

"Not for me, Captain. Here, Eddie, take a look at this."

Adam was looking at a year planner stuck to the wall. Of the three hundred and sixty-five days available, only two were filled. The first in late March said 'Get Pissed', the second in September said 'Possible Shag'. The two men stood in front of the calendar, suppressing their laughter like two school boys at the back of the class, should John overhear.

Adam pointed to the second entry.

"That has just gone; ask him how he got on."

"No."

"Go on."

"Fuck off. Go and send the stop message, 'false alarm, good intent'. I'll have a word with him."

Back in his room, Eddie was completing some paperwork when Linsey knocked.

"Sorry to interrupt, Eddie."

"No problem, Linsey, my door is always open. What can I do you for?"

Eddie wondered if his humorous para jumble could be misconstrued but could tell it hadn't bothered Linsey.

"Just wanted to know what you said to John before you left."

"I told him he was safe, that there was nothing to worry about and we had dealt with it. Asked him if he was ok and told him I knew an expert in this kinda stuff."

"Stuff?"

"Yea, best to be vague and would ask them to pop in and have a chat."

"That expert being social services I guess."

"Got it in one. Don't get involved remember."

"Yea, I…"

Linsey was about to tell Eddie about her visit to Patricia Arnold when the tannoy burst into life.

"Eddie, John wants to know if your free for a drink. Apart from one day next March, he hasn't much on, so give him a bell."

Eddie and Linsey laughed.

"And, Linsey, if your free next September, he wants to know."

Eddie was off his chair and out the room shouting at the culprits before she had the chance to show her amusement.

19

It was Friday and as casual as they all tried to make it, they were looking forward to the retirement drink up this evening.

Harryoo was checking with Jim and Adam if they were taking their wives. 'Yep' was the mutual response. *Nothing worse than being the only one to turn up with the other half*, thought Harry. *Puts things out of kilter*. Doreen would have no one to talk to, which meant his constant attention would be required and that would be a tragedy for Harry while the blokes gathered together for a few beers and a laugh.

"You going tonight, Lazy?"

"Yes, Puke, you?"

"Yea, got a babysitter, first night out for ages. Alice is looking forward to it."

"You bringing anyone, Linsey? I've never asked about your partner."

"No, I'm single at the moment."

"Understandable."

"Ok, let's have it."

"Well, you ain't exactly lady like. That's assuming you're not…"

"What?"

"You know, a bit fidgety."

"You are such a wanker, Luke."

"Why? Look at those hands, fingernails."

They were in the bay testing the airbags.

"What bloke's gonna want them around his todger."

Linsey didn't need to look at her hands to know her blackened fingernails weren't her most attractive feature.

"They'll be around your scrawny neck in a minute. Can't wait to meet Alice tonight and tell her what you just said."

Luke coloured slightly but enough for Linsey to notice.

"Ha, not so cocky now, Puke Dunstford."

"Why are you single, Lins, seriously?"

"Got dumped when I joined the service."

"Really?"

"Yep. Said his mates were taking the piss out of him about having a bird that sleeps with ten men every night when she's working. Get the inference, Luke?"

"'Course. Well, you're better off without that tosser."

"That's what I told myself as I cried into my pillow."

"What in the dorm? I always thought that was Billy."

"Lins."

She turned to see Chris calling her from the door to the watch room.

"ADO wants a word, now."

"Shall I do this first?"

"Better not. Luke can finish up there."

"Typical," said Luke.

Linsey walked across the station to the commander's office. These summons meant only one thing. Patricia Arnold had phoned in a complaint.

She knocked and stepped inside the office, letting the door close on its own. "You wanted to see me, Sir."

Linsey stood, feet apart hands, behind her back in the 'at ease' position.

"Ah, Linsey."

Clarence looked up to see a nervous young firefighter standing barely inside the room.

Been there and know the feeling, he thought before continuing.

"Come in and sit down, Linsey. I don't bite."

She sat on the chair in front of his desk and started.

"Sir, can I just say…"

"Linsey," said Clarence Siddall. "If I may."

Linsey stopped.

"Linsey, I've had a phone call from a Patricia Arnold."

"Sir, it's my…"

"Linsey."

"Yes, Sir."

"Shut up."

"Yes, Sir."

"You attended an incident at her home recently. I don't know how she got this number and I don't want to know. We are ex-directory for a reason, aren't we?"

"Yes, Sir."

"Well, you must have left a good impression because she has asked me to pass on her number to you so she could thank you personally. There we are."

Linsey took the small yellow post-it note.

"Phone her from here, not your own private number. If it is just a thank you she wants to convey, then great. Anything more, then I'd suggest a polite refusal."

Clarence Siddall waited for her reply.

"Yes, Sir."

"Good, don't get involved, Linsey. Everything else ok? Settled in?"

"Yes, Sir. I love it here."

"Good. Are you going to the retirement do tonight?"

"Yes, Sir."

"Good, then I shall see you there and well done."

Eddie was in Arthur Church's room. "I trust you have a little speech prepared for tonight, Guv."

"Yes, thought I'd say a few words."

Eddie knew those few words had been carefully crafted over the past week. John Mullins was adverse to fire service ceremony and tradition but would be quietly pleased that Arthur had taken the time. Time that Arthur really enjoyed taking. He enjoyed, though he would never admit it, public speaking. Especially political rhetoric. Arthur had stood for political office earlier in the year and, though unsuccessful, he would do it again if only for the fun of being on the stump. These little speeches were different but equally enjoyable and important. The balance of humour and praise, reflection and thanks mixed into a valedictory that was not overly long took careful consideration.

Then the hard part, learning it verbatim and giving the impression that without notes, it was being delivered off the cuff. Arthur loved it.

"That will please him," said Eddie.

"Hope so. What did we get him with the whip round?"

"Got him a voucher for the golf shop he uses. I think he will be playing a lot in Spain."

"Do you want me to pick you up?" Arthur asked. "I'm driving, don't mind."

"Thanks, Arthur, but I'm bringing someone and will be driving anyway."

"Ok, I shall look forward to meeting this someone."

"Speaking of driving, Guvnor, couldn't help noticing the new car."

"Yea, thought I'd treat myself. Picked it up two days ago. I know they will say it's my midlife crisis, but hey ho, only a small one."

"Small one, Arthur?"

"Well, a Porsche or Ferrari it is not, so no full-blown crisis."

"Gotcha. Still a nice car and nobody will think that."

In the yard, Perry, Jim, Adam, and Luke stood around the coupe. "These come fully loaded as standard," said Luke.

"Hairdresser's car," said Jim.

"Midlife crisis," offered Adam.

"Definitely," agreed Perry.

It had been a long week for Eddie. He couldn't wait to see Charlotte again and was pleased when she agreed to come this evening. He would meet her off the train and drive to his flat first, so she could drop her overnight bag and freshen up if she needed to. He was peeved to be working the next day and couldn't get out of it but felt better when she informed him that her sister had flown over for a week and she would be spending the weekend at her parents' with her.

"Coming tonight, Sean?" Jim asked as they walked out to the yard for drills.

"Yea, on me own. Never liked taking a bird to a piss up."

Jim, Adam, Perry, and Linsey lined up in front of the tower. Chris stood to one side in the role of safety officer.

Arthur had earlier asked Sean to take Linsey out for drill. It was important that firefighters continued training, more so for recruits.

"Pleasure, Arthur," he had replied.

"Right, that." Sean pointed to the twenty-five litre foam drum. "Is for the purpose of this drill; a cylinder that has been involved in fire and needs to be cooled."

"Firefighter Rivers, how will we deal with it?"

"Is it acetylene?"

"No."

"Set up a ground monitor."

"No. You haven't considered water run off."

"Make a shallow dam."

"At last. I want you to construct the dam. Tell the rest of the crew what you need. Chaps, just assist please, let her tie all knots. Ok, get to work."

Linsey got the triple extension ladder off the lorry and, with Perry's help, created a triangle. As it lay on its side, she lashed it together with a long line while answering a barrage of questions from Sean Stolly.

"How long is the long line?" She told him.

"How heavy is the triple ex?" She told him.

"What knots are you using?" She told him.

Linsey laid the heavy-duty salvage sheet inside the triangle she had created and tied it off. She then ran out a length of hose from the pump and into her shallow dam. The pump had been engaged, and the hydrant set in by Jim, Adam, and Perry. Linsey immediately opened the delivery valve and started filling the dam with water.

"Fuck sake. Knock off!" Sean Stolly screamed.

Linsey quickly knocked the revs off the pump. She had forgotten to weigh the end of the hose that lay in the dam. With the revs from the pump too high, the hose flew out of the dam, soaking Sean Stolly.

"Sorry, Sean." She could see Chris Everett laughing; so could Sean, which increased his anger.

"Some fucking safety officer," his said as he walked past Chris.

"Fucking sorry ain't good enough. That hose was out of control and that's fucking dangerous. What should you have done?"

"Weighed it down."

"What with?"

"Er…" Before she could suggest a dividing breaching. Sean continued his tirade.

"Er, fucking er won't weigh it down. Get it weighed down, get the dam filled, and the cylinder in it. Get to work."

At the end of the drill, the four firefighters were making up the equipment. Sean Stolly walked over to Chris.

"Keep an eye on them, Safety Officer. I'm going to get dry fire gear."

"Bit harsh on her, Sean," said Chris.

"Fucking harsh. Mistakes like that cause injuries. I wouldn't have let her out of training school."

He turned to walk away.

"Or you."

"What was that?" Chris asked.

"Nuffin." Sean carried on walking off the drill yard.

"Was it that bad?" Linsey asked Adam, Jim, and Perry as they removed their fire gear.

"No," said Adam. "Don't worry about it. I guess he didn't like getting a soaking from the sprog."

Perry chipped in. "He's old school. Thinks you will remember a bollocking on the drill ground and won't repeat it on the fire ground."

"I done the same thing to my first sub officer," said Jim. "Took him off his feet."

"Oh, did you get a bollocking?"

"What do you think? Come on, it's lunch." With that, he ran to the mess, followed by Perry and Adam.

"You ok, Linsey?" She was joined by Chris.

"Yes, thanks, Chris. Sorry, did I get you in trouble?"

"Huh, he doesn't trouble me, Linsey, and don't let him trouble you. That won't happen again when I'm on duty."

Linsey nodded her appreciation and, not knowing what had passed between the two leading firefighters, was a little surprised and heartened by Chris' disdain.

20

Charlotte walked into Eddie's flat.

"Bedroom, I'll put your bag in here. Toilet, and this is the open plan lounge and kitchen."

Eddie opened up his balcony, keen to show her the sea glimpse that he had. "It's lovely, Ed."

She considered the bland white and grey colour scheme in the lounge interrupted by a large wall canvas consisting of a metallic orange background on which black concentric circles had been painted. The TV was the biggest she'd ever seen. Another wall had a, what she assumed, football shirt in a glass-fronted frame. Next to that were two shelves of books. She ran her fingers along the spines and was surprised by the eclectic mix of Steinbeck, Larkin, and Waugh. The kitchen was empty. "Do you cook for yourself, Ed?"

"Sure. I haven't done anything for us this evening as I'm reliably informed there is a buffet, but I have plenty for breakfast."

"Coddled eggs?"

Eddie took her in his arms and kissed her.

"Your wish is my command."

Linsey started to get ready. She thought about phoning Patricia before making her way to Cloud Nein, but decided against it. If she were asked to meet tonight, she would have to refuse, and she didn't want to seem negative in any way.

She was nervous, too. Had she bitten off more than she could chew? Would Patricia make demands of her that she couldn't fulfil? Why didn't she just listen to her bosses? Anyway, forget about it tonight. She was looking forward to meeting all the partners. She had tried before to imagine Alice Dunstford, poor woman, and Ken's Thai bride, Chimlin, whom he adored. Billy was single and a very private man. Maybe she would find out more this evening over a beer.

Adam, Jim, Perry, and Harryoo all socialised together outside of work. That might not be an easy clique to join.

Arthur was a widower. *Must be tough,* she thought, and should she mention it? Chris, lovely Chris. If his partner, Jamie, were half as nice as him, then it would be a pleasure to get acquainted. She overheard that Eddie had a new girlfriend. Bet she's gorgeous. The only fly in the ointment was Sean Stolly. Surely, he wouldn't be obnoxious in mixed company. She'd stay out of his way.

Cloud Nein occupied a corner plot in a row of shops at the top of the hill. Between the bar and the bridge that led to the train station was The Railway Tavern. On weekends, customers would have a couple in there first before slipping next door for bottled beer and cocktails. The one transgression from the house style was draught Stella. The owner had been advised early on that the male clientele would generally forgive the absence of their favourite tipple when offered the Flemish lager as a substitute, and the advice had been proved correct.

The owner of Cloud Nein was Austrian. One of the reasons he loved the UK was the British humour, which he had tried to imitate when he named his bar. On one occasion, a customer mentioned it, he was left bemused.

"This your bar, mate?"

"Yes, it is."

"You're foreign, ain't ya?"

"That's right, I am."

"Thought so, you spelt nine wrong. Cheers."

As the man sauntered to a table, Jonas couldn't decide if he had just experienced that humour or a vacant local.

Being on a corner, Jonas could create three distinct areas in Cloud Nein. The general bar where customers first entered. To the right of that, a rectangular space that could be cleared for dancing and off that space, around the back, a smaller bar only opened on really busy nights.

This was the space John Mullins had taken over for the evening. He was leaning on the bar with his beer when his first guests arrived.

"Evening, Ken." They shook hands.

"Hallo, Chimlin." John bent down and kissed her on the cheek.

"What you having?"

John heard the front door go and Jim's laugh, which had been one of the soundtracks to his time on the Red.

Jim and Emma, Adam and Marianne walked around the corner.

"Whey!"

"Hiya!"

"Hallo!"

"John."

The greetings were repeated.

Adam clapped Ken on the shoulder. "Knew you'd get here first. What's that, your second or third?"

Ken was about to tell him to fuck off but Adam had moved on and was kissing Chimlin.

It was then that Ken realised a serious flaw in the evening.

"John, free bar, ain't it?"

"Yea."

"Panic over, Ken," said Jim to everyone's amusement.

Ken ignored the comment.

"How you going to stop some Herbert sneaking around here and ordering for free, should the word get out?"

"Ah, glad you reminded me, Ken."

John pulled out a handful of red wristbands from his pocket. "Please take one each, then order what you want. Barman sees that, he knows you're with me."

"Good thinking," said Adam, taking one.

"Down there for dancing," said John.

Chimlin watched John point to his shoes, then looked at Ken quizzically.

"I'll explain later, darling."

Within the hour, all had arrived bar one. Charlotte had been introduced and had whispered to Eddie that she would never remember all the names except Harryoo's.

The old joke had broken the ice with the formal greetings.

"Hi, I'm Charlotte."

"Good evening, Charlotte. I'm Harryoo."

"Harryoo!"

"Fine, thanks. How are you?"

The men laughed; the women groaned.

"See what we have to put up with," said Doreen.

"That's just the start," said Billy. "He has a full repertoire of corny jokes."

"And when he starts, just walk away," said Jim.

Eddie guided her through the throng to Arthur. He was the only man in a jacket and tie, his stoop pronounced as he stood over the buffet contemplating a vol au vent.

"Charlotte, I'd like you to meet my guvnor, Arthur."

Arthur gave a slight jump as his concentration was broken.

"Arthur, Charlotte."

"This is a pleasure. I've heard so much about you," he lied.

"Really?" She gave Eddie a sideways glance.

"Indeed, you have become his one topic of conversation."

"Ok, now I know you're making fun of me."

"Heaven forfend. You work in the National Gallery. I used to pop in there a lot when I was stationed at Soho."

"Another fan of Extract Depressionists, no doubt," Charlotte said, assuming she was still being played.

Arthur's confused gaze turned briefly towards the ceiling as he considered yet another esoteric art movement he was unaware of.

It was at this point that Charlotte realised Arthur was on the level.

"Or Turner, perhaps," she suggested, wanting to make amends.

Arthur shielded his mouth from Eddie.

"Don't tell anyone but I love the still life paintings of flowers by the old Dutch masters."

"Then, we have much in common, art and vol au vents."

"Well, not that one," he said, pointing to the table. "It looks old enough to have been in a Jan Van whoever."

"De Heem," suggested Charlotte.

"That's him."

"I'll just go and get some drinks," announced Eddie. "What would you like, Charlotte?"

"A…" She turned towards the bar. "Gin and tonic, please, not too much ice."

"Arthur?"

"No, I'm fine, thanks."

Eddie sidled up to John, who was talking to his brother.

"Ah, Eddie, here." John placed two wristbands in his hand.

"Not that I can imagine Charlotte wearing it."

"Reason being?" Eddie asked.

"No offence, mate, but Charlotte doesn't strike me as the type of woman who goes to venues that require wristbands or hand stamps."

The high windows along the back wall had been opened for fresh air. A through train to London could be heard in its hurry.

"Other side of the tracks," said John.

Earlier today, Eddie had sneaked a peek at Arthur's speech. John always spoke truth to power was the phrase Eddie remembered. John spoke the truth to everyone, he thought.

"Well, she's definitely slumming it tonight, and she said as you're paying, she is going to cane the gin."

"Well, I can't imagine her using that phrase, but please tell her she is more than welcome."

It was now that the last person to arrive arrived.

The women noticed first. Especially Jim's wife, Emma, who was pregnant and felt vulnerable and unattractive. Whether it was the infinitesimal rise in pheromone or the apprehensive stare on the faces of their men, it would be neither here nor there later when, on the way home or in bed, the interrogations began.

"So, plain Jane, eh?"

"Is her bed next to yours?"

"Looks like a lump of lard, does she?"

"What made you think she's a lesbian?"

Harryoo was in the biggest trouble. He had failed to mention to Doreen that the new recruit was a female.

Linsey, stung by Luke's comments, had decided to make an effort. In the bath, she soaked and scrubbed her hands before applying a crimson nail varnish to match her lipstick. She wore black. Black stiletto ankle boots, black skinny jeans, and a black four-button blouse with a high collar and deep cleavage. The sleeves were three-quarter length. A necklace, a broad band of loose-fitting steel, interrupted one's gaze from Linsey's neck to her ample cleavage. Her ears, not visible behind her long blonde hair, were unadorned, and in her hand she carried a purse large enough for maybe her keys, lipstick, and bank card. It actually contained two twenty-pound notes and a knife with three blades. Her car key and door key were in her pocket.

The walk from car to bar was not long, but the cold night air had excited a light pink blush to her cheeks. The moisture captured in her eyes shone in the barroom lights.

"Hallo, you must be Alice. It's so nice to meet you. Luke is always talking about you and the children."

"Positively, I hope."

Linsey read the look on Puke's face. It said quite clearly, 'say the wrong thing now and I'll never forgive you' and in that moment, she realised that the balance of power had for one night shifted in her favour.

"Of course, totally devoted. Let me say hi to everyone and get a drink. Speak to you later yea."

Linsey worked the room. She congratulated Emma and asked Marianne about her children. She commiserated with Perry and Rachel regarding the loss of their dog. She had heard Harry could give Doreen a hard time, so she couldn't resist when saying hallo with a peck on his cheek.

"Fuck me, he's in trouble," said Adam to Jim.

"You are very beautiful," said Chimlin.

"Oh, that's kind of you. That makes two of us, then."

"Do you like working at the fire station?" Chimlin asked.

"Yes, especially with Ken. He is like my second father and the best cook." Ken straightened his back and pulled in his belly as he looked with pride at his two beauties.

Billy told her she scrubbed up nice as he met her going to the bar. "Want a drink?"

"Thanks, Bill, arf a lager shandy ta."

"Enjoying yourself," said Jamie.

"Yea, nice bunch," said Linsey.

Chris arrived with drinks.

"Here you go, Billy sent this. This is my partner, Jamie. Jamie, this is Linsey."

"So I gathered," said Jamie. "Nice to meet you, darling, and I've particularly enjoyed watching the carnage you've left in your wake so far this evening."

"Really? Don't know what you're talking about."

"Except Eddie and Charlotte, you never lingered there." Linsey gave a conspiratorial shake of the head.

"Untouchable," she said.

The three smiled together, initiating their gang.

"Are you leaving the men to their own devices?" Jamie said, nodding in the direction of a large group of men that included firefighters from across the county, John, his brother, and Sean Stolly.

"Yea, I never really got to know John and…"

For the first time since her arrival, she faltered, so quickly changed the subject.

"Chris told me you are air crew?"

"Cabin crew, yes, darling."

Chris had started a conversation with Perry.

"When I get back from a trip, he can't wait to tell me everything."

"Really, that's nice."

Jamie pulled his mojito through the paper straw.

"Everything. He was disappointed when John resigned, and lately his discontent has been compounded."

Linsey understood but was reluctant to concur. Chris was one of her line managers, and she didn't want to say something inappropriate that would get back to him. She was relieved when Jamie resumed.

"Occasionally, on a flight, we get a complete arsehole."

Jamie took a step closer to Linsey as he took her in his confidence. Linsey thought he smelled fantastic.

"You know the type, macho man, loud, and bigoted, clearly homophobic. Snide comments from the start."

Linsey waited for Jamie to continue. He didn't. He waited for her question. "What do you do?"

"I get in their face." Jamie held her gaze. A third party not privy to their conversation could reasonably deduce she was being admonished.

"I think 'Right, I'm the only person on the plane that's dealing with you, buster'. I start with easy, quiet words, don't show yourself up: 'I understand how some MEN are afraid of flying and self-sedate with alcohol, but there is aviation law and should I deem you have broken one, then you'll be regretting this flight for a long time'. Then, throughout the flight, he gets my immediate attention. The seatbelt sign comes on. I go to him first to check that he is complying. When I remove his empty coffee cup, I tap my pockets and wonder out loud where I put the laxative pills. His neighbours laugh. Laugh at him. If I meet him in the aisle, I make him stand aside. Never take a backwards step, never. That guy is usually glad to get off the plane."

Linsey took in this slender, effete, handsome man and considered how looks can be deceiving.

"Most bullies are cowards, Linsey. Another drink?" He asked, taking her glass. Without a beer in her hand, Linsey suddenly felt awkward, ill at ease. As she pondered Jamie's approach to intimidation, she watched him make his way to the bar. He went straight to the end occupied by the group of men surrounding John, who was holding court. It was as he squeezed past them, she noticed Sean Stolly staring at her. She forced a smile and gave a waist-high wave. His features remained impassive as he eyed her up and down. It reminded her of the look her brother had when inspecting a side of beef. He then slugged his drink and, wiping his mouth with the back of his hand, he turned back to the group.

Conversation politely bubbled across the room until Arthur stilled the frothy confab, tapping the side of his glass with a spoon. It was time for the speech.

"John, could you join me please and, Mr Barman, if you wouldn't mind shutting the bar for ten minutes?"

Eddie and Charlotte had made their way to the border, where the small bar joined the larger dance floor. They had been chatting to Clarence Siddall and his partner, Clare, when the retirement party had been brought to order. They listened as Arthur began regaling the gathered throng with John's well-documented faux pas'. Eddie had slipped his arm around Charlotte's waist and pulled her close. She hooked her thumb in his back pocket while running her fingers lightly over his bum. Eddie was really enjoying the evening. Charlotte was a natural in company. She possessed the poise of an ambassador and the charm of a seasoned host. Then later, back to his, perfect.

"Arthur is being rather harsh on John," observed Charlotte, her lips close to his ear.

"Exactly what John would have hoped. The level of piss taking reflects the personality. Well-liked characters get the most."

Charlotte put her other hand on his shoulder and whispered, "Ken must be a popular guy." Eddie smiled.

"Eddie, Uncle Ed."

A familiar voice not heard for a while startled him. He turned. "Charlotte, hallo." He breathed the words, not wanting to interrupt Arthur. Charlotte thought he seemed embarrassed to see her.

A round of applause signalled the end of the presentations. "Er…" He looked nervously from Charlotte to Charlotte. "Charlotte, meet Charlotte."

Charlotte thrust out her hand. "Hi ya, are you Eddie's…" She was not sure what to say next.

Charlotte took over. "Yes."

"Lovely name."

"Thanks, you too." Eddie took over.

"What you doing here? Thought you were at uni."

"I am; I recently started my third year."

"Okay."

"Come home as much as I can now since dad had the stroke."

"No, Charlotte!" Eddie exclaimed. "How is he? How bad?"

"Where do I start? Very limited use down his right side. Vision problems and his speech…"

Tear's brimmed as she looked away from them both.

"He has trouble saying things, what he wants, choosing the right words, his brain is confused."

The older Charlotte reached into her bag and gave her younger namesake a tissue.

"Thanks."

Eddie's embrace was met with a rejecting arch of the back. He let go.

"I never knew, Charlotte. I'm so sorry."

"Why would you, Uncle Eddie?"

His honorary title was spoken with a barbed inflexion.

"You never phone, never go to the shop. How would you know?"

"I've, er…been busy, Charlotte, moving my dad back to London and…" He was sounding pathetic, so he decided to let the rest of his sentence hang in space.

"Your mum, how is she?"

"How do you think? She's devastated and exhausted."

"I'll…"

"Yea, do, it would mean a lot. Anyhow, I'm meeting some friends, gotta go. It was nice meeting you, Charlotte, bye."

With the completion of the presentations, Jonas assumed it a good idea to provide music for John's free drinking group. He thought by getting them in the party spirit, they would stick around and exhaust John's funds. What nobody had explained to Jonas was at retirement do's, people came to talk. It was a time to see old faces, catch up, to listen, to tell, to laugh. The aural inhibitor emanating from the speakers irritated the company that had to raise their voices to be heard.

So, the vagaries of the night sap the spirit and the comfort of home calls. Drinks are diluted by slushy ice, beer acquires a vinegar tang, fragrance is soured on clammy skin, and thoughts of tomorrow and its duties become paramount. Children and hangovers, work and hangovers, hangovers. The party of colleagues and casual acquaintances start to disperse. Hands are shook and cheeks kissed.

"We must meet up."

"Nice to see you."

"It's been too long."

Society demands the platitudes to which everyone acquiesces. It's just John with his tumbler full of whiskey and a couple of die-hard blokes off the leash who remain.

"Good luck in Spain, John. Hasta la vista."

"Goodbye, John, and thanks. It has been a blast but we have to go."

To the disappointment of Jonas, the bar emptied.

21

Eddie and Charlotte lay on his settee. Their clothes, in a trail of seduction, lay along the hallway into the living room.

"Sorry, beauty, but I need the loo."

Eddie sat up and slipped into his boxers before padding back into the hallway, picking up clothes as he went. Upon his return, Charlotte had dressed.

He took her hands.

"Come to bed and I can undress you all over again."

She pulled him down next to her and kissed him.

"Hmm, toothpaste."

"Had to get rid of my beery breath."

"I might like beery breath on a man."

"Do you?"

"Well, it's a new one for me."

"What, didn't your old man drink?"

"Ed, we are not going to talk about my ex every time we make love."

"Ok, let's make love again and I promise not to mention him."

"Make me a coffee, Ed."

"Coffee! At this time."

"Yes, please. I'm not ready for the night to end just yet. I want you to talk to me, it's your turn."

"Talk about what?" Eddie was in the kitchen preparing the coffee.

Staring across his open plan apartment, Charlotte was trying to make out the words that were wrapped in an elaborate design on the back of his tee shirt. "Does that say territorial pissing?"

"Yea, sorry, first one out of the draw."

"Why on earth would you buy it?" Eddie was frothing the milk.

"Weekend in Brussels, stag do. Bridegroom's stupid drunk brother decides to squirt tomato sauce over everyone, me mainly. Shirt ruined. I go into the first shop I see, saw this white tee, bought it in a hurry without looking at the back. The moronic brother thought it was cool and has nagged me for it ever since."

"Please give it to him."

Eddie brought over the coffee.

"It's alright for bed."

"Well, it's coming off."

"If you insist."

"First, though, Eddie, tell me why a good-looking, intelligent and funny guy with a good job, own place, is single?"

"Tell me who it is and I'll have a stab."

"Don't prevaricate, Eddie, and stop hiding behind humour. I can understand if wedlock doesn't appeal but surely, there has been one meaningful long-term relationship."

Why do women need to know everything? he thought. *Just because they find it easy wearing their hearts on a sleeve, we have to as well.*

"Eddie."

She ran hers fingers through his hair above his ear. He placed his hand on her bare leg then looked her in the eye.

"It's the second part of that word that has undesirable connotations for me."

"What word?"

"Wedlock. My parents were locked in a marriage that neither wanted."

"Why? Because of you?"

"Yes, and duty, and solemn vows, till death do us part."

"You make them sound Victorian."

"They were probably the last generation with those ingrained beliefs before the swinging sixties blew it all away."

"Was it an unhappy home?"

"Strangely enough, no. My mother was a force of nature, never a quiet moment when she was around, and dad was…" Eddie thought for a moment.

"He was dull but in a way that didn't offend."

Charlotte thought she had never heard such a damming indictment of a man's character.

"So, marriage is an outmoded concept for you?"

"Not outmoded, plenty make a success of it, but for me, no."

"Ever lived with someone?"

"Nope."

"That's a serious lack of commitment."

Eddie removed his hand.

"You make me sound cold. I'm not."

She sensed his defences slide in between them and acted quickly, kissing him, before they hardened into a fortification.

"You're lovable, and I'm sure I'm not the only woman to have thought that. Tell me more about Jane."

Christ, he felt like a boy with a secret when he heard a knock on the door and the voice of a policeman asking if Eddie Hart lived here. He had given Charlotte a vague outline of his relationship with the Hobsons in the car home, but her feminine intuition and the young Charlotte's admonishment aroused her curiosity.

"I've told ya. More coffee?"

"Come on, your turn tonight."

Eddie pressed his back into the settee and looked at the ceiling.

"We knew one another at school. Jane would come to my house. She loved my mum. I went off to sea and that was that. Next time I saw her, she was married to Nev. Charlotte is their only child. Jane has a hairdressers. One day, my mum walks in for a hairdo, and that rekindled their friendship. Charlotte loved my mum also, and I would get a haircut from time to time. That's it." Now he realised he did sound cold.

"Now, poor old Nev has had a stroke, so I need to give them a call and see if I can do anything."

Charlotte took his coffee cup and went to the kitchen area. She found the dishwasher and placed the china in the top rack. The work top was immaculately clean and empty. She found a dishcloth, made it wet, and started to wipe the surfaces.

She thought about the dunnage, all the old wood that is dragged through life from one alliance to the next and splinters that have to be prised out along the way before they turn septic. In hindsight, her load to bear was straightforward. Her husband wanted kids, but she couldn't provide, so he left for someone who could. Eddie, on the other hand, may have a heavier burden. The consequences of a bad marriage, handed down or an empty chamber of the heart, chained and padlocked, the key lost.

She felt his arm around her. He kissed her neck, then brushed his lips over her ear.

She wanted him but felt she was sailing through a fog worried about unseen flotsam and the damage it may cause.

22

A Saturday at work after a night out was not the worse place to be. Most of the Red would rather risk a hard-working job accompanied by a hangover than face weekend shopping, kids' playgrounds, or long-standing DIY.

The night shift hadn't turned a wheel. Nothing required doing, they sat around the mess table reading papers or engaged in idle chat about the day's sport and how good the night out had been.

"John enjoyed it."

"S'main fing."

"He was well on his way when we left."

"Who've the ammers got today?"

Linsey was the last to join the group. She had caught some traffic on the way to work and had to phone in late travelling.

"Morning all." She took a mug of tea from the aluminium tray.

"What time do you call this?"

"Couldn't get out of yer pit."

"Hungover from last night."

She ignored the barbed comments.

"Sorry, Guv." She looked at Arthur, who smiled back. "One lane out cos of flooding."

"You should plan for all eventualities. Ain't that right, Guv?"

A gentle ripple of laughter went around the table. Harryoo was late more often than the rest of the watch put together.

"Thanks, Harry, I'll remember that."

"He's getting you back for that kiss last night."

"What kiss?" A perplexed Ken asked.

"Don't worry, Ken. No tongues," chipped in Perry.

"I should hope not," he replied. "Can't have kissing on the watch; don't know where it will end up."

"Don't worry, Ken, I'm not that sort of girl."

"Humph."

Sean pushed out the noise without looking up from his paper.

Linsey let it go.

"Did you get any grief from Doreen?" Adam asked Harry.

"Why?"

"Over the kiss."

"No, Doreen and I trust one another completely," said Harry as seriously as he could manage.

"Dor probably took one look at Lins," said Billy to general approval, "and knew aitch would never stand a chance."

"Aw, thanks, Billy," said Linsey.

"Yea, thanks, Bill," said Harry.

"I should think not," said Ken.

It was Luke's turn.

"Why did you turn up like that anyway?"

"Like what?" She asked.

"You know, all…" Luke thought through his descriptive lexicon. "All tarted up."

"All tarted up!" She exclaimed.

Luke looked around the table for support. None was forthcoming. Despite the comments that some had received late last night from their respective, the firefighters knew that remark went too far, plus three of the four officers had varying degrees of rebuke plastered across their faces. Sean Stolly carried on reading.

Luke caved.

"Sorry, Lins, but you know."

"No, not really."

Linsey was annoyed with Luke. As much as she liked him, she could do without judgment like that, especially in front of Sean.

"Before you came out last night, didn't you shower and slap on some aftershave?"

"I doubt if he did," said Harry.

"Fuck off, aitch."

"Obviously not as secure in your marriage as I am." Harryoo loved the moral high ground.

Billy was enjoying the banter. He answered to no one.

"I thought you looked lovely, Linsey."

His comment was met with general disdain, but it broke the ice.

"Oh, I thought you looked lovely too, Linsey."

"Yea, the way you, the way you combed your hair, lovely."

"And your lippy, what was it?"

"Lippy! Numb nuts."

"I liked your handbag."

They were on a roll. The slight forgotten. Linsey was laughing, eager to join in.

"Oh, that's my favourite lippy. I'll bring some in."

Her sentence was interrupted by a fire call.

23

Rain had fallen steadily all night. From midnight till dawn, the heavens provided a downpour akin to the hotel that boasted an en suite with a tropical rain shower.

The fields that ringed Langden absorbed what water they could, but the task proved too much, so it ran wild. Down the hills through and around woodland, down culverts and streams, down farm tracks and bridle paths, down pathways and gardens, always down, then through. Through gates, through gaps under doors, through vents and grates, through air bricks and cat flaps. Nothing sought out the low life like a deluge of water looking for somewhere to rest.

The trick when confronted with an overwhelming force is to outsmart it. Only stand in front of a grizzly bear knowing there is a hidden bear pit between you and the beast. The skill required when challenged with flooding is to send it on its way. Keep it moving like an invading army passing through the unwelcome shuttered village. Essential to this stratagem is pre-planning. Well-designed storm drains maintained rivulets, streams, and irrigation ditches. Keep the muddy water moving.

The new generation of residents in Low Street had worked hard to bring the old farm cottages and weatherboard bungalows into the twenty-first century. They had added garages and block paved the front gardens. They could enjoy a rural idyll, safe in the knowledge that civilisation was a mere two miles away. The only fly, or more accurately, mosquito, in their ointment was the irrigation ditch in front of their homes. Overgrown with weeds most of the year and a stagnant breeding ground for midges in the summer, like the farm cockerel, it was proving to be an irritant that had to go. Although not belonging to them, it was gradually filled with unwanted earth from redesigned driveways and general garden waste. What could go wrong?

Whether it was a one in a hundred year flood or one in fifty for the residents of Low Street, one of the more extreme elements of nature had decided this morning to visit them. Devoid of help from the ditch, the road was subsumed by 0930 hours. Five minutes later, as the water lapped at their thresholds, the residents of Low Street started to call for help.

"Control said they are getting multiple calls of flooding," said Chris, coming off the red phone.

"Ok," said Arthur.

The red phone was the direct line to the staff at HQ, who mobilised all appliances.

"So, we might not get immediate support if needed."

Arthur took the tip sheet from Chris and read it.

"What we got?" Eddie asked.

"Low Street, flooding."

A flood like a snow drift changes a familiar landscape. Gone are the clearly defined features, and with that goes the confidence when traversing an area of unseen impediments.

"Careful where you walk, Lins," said Adam as they alighted from the appliance.

"Don't want to go under like the Vicar of Dibley."

Of the two, water is the evil twin. A pristine covering of white is considered beautiful by most. Untamed water, on the other hand, is society's nightmare, and it never comes alone. A slurry of manure, chemicals, and sewage more often than not tags along for the ride.

The rescue pump and water tender had pulled up at the water's edge. Thankfully, the rain had stopped, and the sun was out. Arthur waved to the residents as they desperately tried to defend their island homes. He turned to Eddie.

"If that ditch has not been completely filled in, we may be able to set in and start pumping the water to Woolifers. I noticed the stream there was full but running freely. Use the light portable pump."

"Sounds like a plan, Stan." Eddie started barking at the crews.

With the operation underway, Eddie called Linsey over to him.

"Alright, Linsey?"

"Yes, thanks, Eddie."

"Did you enjoy last night?"

"Yea, it was nice putting faces to all the names and Charlotte is lovely."

"Yea, listen about this morning with Luke. I'll have a word."

"No, please don't, Eddie. It's fine. I like Luke, we're good."

"I don't want you to think you have to put up with sexist behaviour, that goes for Arthur too."

"Thank you. Look, I have two older brothers. I'm used to male comments, male humour; I'm used to men. I'm no shrinking Violet. If Luke or any of the watch upset me, I'll let 'em know. I can give as good as I get." Arthur joined them.

"The water level hasn't risen. I've been to all the properties and the damage is minimal, so I'm gonna send a detaining message, say we might be here another two hours."

"Ok, Guv. Linsey and I have been talking."

Arthur watched over the people within his command with a benign authority.

He presided over the dynamics of the group, only stepping in when necessary, content with the knowledge that reasonable adults policed themselves. A rebuke from one's peers often carried more weight than one from a higher power. Looking at Eddie and Linsey's demeanour, he knew the house was in order.

"Good," he replied, walking away.

'What's for lunch?' asked the firefighters as they descended on the mess room. The Red had been out all morning and had missed the stand easy. They were famished.

"Salad," said Harry, laying the table.

"Salad, fucking salad. I am literally starving, and you give me salad."

"Jim, you are not literally starving, far from it. Gretchen is off today, and I didn't know how long you'd be out, so, yes, salad with a choice of pork pie or smoked mackerel fillets."

Ken had entrusted Harry with the messing.

"Can we have both?" Perry asked.

"If you share."

"I ain't sharing nuffin."

"Have we got spuds?"

"Yes!"

"And the baguettes from the stand easy."

"Yes!"

They began to calm down.

"The fresh beetroot is delicious," said Chris.

"Don't eat beetroot, it scares me," said Jim.

Chris laughed. "Ok, why?"

"Eat that stuff, then when you crap, it looks like you got bowel cancer." A bemused Chris looked at Eddie. Eddie shrugged his shoulders.

Chris and Harryoo were riding the ALP. They had been out messing and had then prepared the food. Harry was filling the mugs. Tea slopped onto the aluminium tray.

"I had such a huge baguette at eleven that I'm still stuffed, so my pie is up for negotiation," he stated.

Most of them were sitting around the table.

Adam looked at Jim.

"Don't give him the satisfaction," he muttered under his breath.

"Stand firm, Jimmy boy," suggested Perry.

Jim looked at his plate of food. This was it until he got home tonight: a smallish pie, a few spuds and some leaves. That evening meal with Emma and the kids was a distant horizon.

"What do you want for it?" He asked.

"The ALP both nights."

"Don't," said Billy.

"One night."

"Both."

Arthur joined the table.

"What's going on?"

"Tense negotiations," said Sean.

Jim had already given Harry both days. For nothing. He had swapped the ALP for the busy bus. Jim liked going out the doors, but at night, that was different. Riding the ALP was a chance of two nights in bed, at least a better chance than if you were driving the water tender.

"No deal."

"Well done, Son," said Ken.

"One night."

"Ok, done."

Perry and Billy laughed. Arthur shook his head.

"Jim," rebuked Adam.

"Got to keep my energy levels up, mate."

Adam nodded. He understood.

Outside at the back of the bay, Luke was using the high-pressure hose on Linsey's fire boots. She held one leg up like a horse being shod as he blasted the mud out of the tread.

Before she could reciprocate, Luke apologised again.

"Forget it, alright."

"It's just Alice, well…" He was hesitant.

"Well, what?"

"I think she got a bit, you know. Asking questions about the dorm and stuff."

"That's crazy. What's she worried about?"

"Well, it's different in this job, ya know the nights."

"Luke, men and women work together all over this country, in offices, factories, hospitals, ambulances, police cars."

"Alright, I get the message."

"Good, doesn't matter about the bloody nights."

"Really!"

"Look, if two people are gonna shag, they are going to do it no matter where they are. Do you want me to talk to Alice?"

"No! Fuck sake."

"I'm happy to tell her I wouldn't touch you with a ten-foot barge pole."

"Won't be necessary, cos I wouldn't touch you with one."

The two friends looked at one another and smiled.

"Come on," said Linsey, taking the hose off him. "Leg up."

Eddie was on the blower.

"Dad, dad, hallo dad."

"Who is this?"

"Who is it? It's me, Eddie."

"Hi, Son. What do you want?"

"I'm fine, thanks. How are you?"

Eddie was in his room. He sat down on his bed and leant back against the wall. He waited for a reply.

"Dad, are you alright?"

He could hear Ray laughing.

"What you laughing at, Dad?"

"Telly."

Ray sounded vague. Non compos mentis.

"Dad, are you in pain?"

"Nope."

"Have you taken pills, Dad?"

"Nope."

"Dad, you don't sound right. I'm calling…"

"No pills, no pain, just whiskey."

"Dad, are you pissed?"

"Bit."

"Fuck sake, Dad, it's just midday. How much you had?"

"All of it."

"You've finished the bottle I brought."

"Yep."

Eddie knew there was half a bottle left from their recent housewarming drink. "It's the poor man's heroin, Son; not the poor man's, the legal man's heroin. That's what it is, legal man's. Takes away the pain and gives a nice buzz. Yea, that's it, nice buzz."

"Have you eaten?"

"Yea, bread."

"With what?"

"Nothin just bread, two slices."

This was a perplexing development for Eddie. Ray enjoyed a tot. Never half a bottle and by lunchtime.

"Dad, are you wearing a shirt with a breast pocket?"

"Er, no, two breast pockets."

"Good. When we hang up, I want you to place the phone in your breast pocket."

"Which one?"

"Doesn't matter. You haven't put it on silent, have you?"

"What's that?"

"Never mind, just place it in your breast pocket. I'm phoning again in about two hours. To check you're ok. I'll come up tonight."

"It's ok, you know. I'm ok; not senile, just pissed. I'm allowed to get pissed, Son."

"Yes, Dad, and I'm allowed to be concerned."

"Oh, sorry, Sean, I was looking for Arthur."

Linsey had mistaken Sean's 'come in' for the guvnor's when she knocked on the door.

He stood at the station officer's desk, casually turning the pages of the standing orders.

"He won't be a minute." Sean gave a cursory nod to the closed door.

The room had en suite facilities referred to in the time-honoured trope as RHIP. Rank has its privileges.

Her hand still on the door handle, she started to back out of the room.

"I'll come back later."

"So, enjoying last night's notoriety." She felt abashed by the comment.

"I enjoyed last night, but notoriety no. Why do you say that?"

"Notoriety," he repeated his accusation as if she didn't understand its meaning.

"What, why?"

He looked up from the desk.

"Well, the jury's verdict this morning was quite clear."

"Sean, I…"

The door opened, and Arthur stepped into the room.

"A queue, I must be getting popular."

"Have you got the drill records, Guv? I thought I'd incorporate this morning's job with a bit of make-believe. If that's ok."

"Over there, Sean, and thanks."

Sean picked up the watch's training records and slipped past Linsey with a smile. "No rest for the wicked," he said.

Linsey pushed herself against the door frame, not wanting any contact as Sean departed.

"Linsey, everything alright?"

Arthur was now seated at his desk, his latest novel in hand. The bookmark indicated he was approaching midway.

"Can I use your phone, Guv? It's official."

"Well, if it's official, you won't mind me asking why."

Linsey explained what had transpired with Patricia Arnold and how Clarence Siddall had told her to deal with it.

She had been thinking about Patricia since the conversation with the ADO and decided that he was right, and so too was Eddie. She had been naive to think she could take matters into her own hands and improve them. She would phone Patricia, hear what she had to say, and receive her thanks, hopefully. Linsey then thought, before concluding the conversation with her, of saying something along the lines of not hesitating to call if she needed us in the future. That, she thought, would be that, thereby putting the whole awkward experience behind her.

Arthur opened the tome and placed the treasured bookmark on the desk that his late wife had bought him at the Hay literary festival.

"I think you'll find the ADO's office is never locked. Use his phone."

"I can use his office, Guv?"

Linsey sounded as if she had just been granted access to the inner sanctum of the Star Chamber.

"Yes, Linsey. The ADO told you how to deal with the matter, I'm telling you to use his phone. Now, I've got approximately half an hour left of my lunchtime."

Arthur leant back in his chair and smiled.

"If you wouldn't mind."

Harryoo's face appeared next to the door jamb.

"Guv, do you want..."

"Out."

"Yes, Guv, laters."

Linsey and Harry walked away from the office.

"You upset him, Lins?"

"No! He wants to read his book."

"Books." Harry sniffed contemptuously at the thought of such a boring pastime.

"What was you gonna ask him? If it ain't personal like."

Harryoo looked round making sure they weren't overheard.

"I noticed he didn't eat his pork pie. It's on the side in the kitchen. If he don't want it, I thought I might have it."

"I heard you got the first night on the ALP. Going for the second, are we?"

"Linsey! I'm hurt. Don't like seeing good food go to waste."

Jim was walking towards them about to ascend the stairs to the TV room. He was carrying a mug of tea and eating a pork pie.

"Is that Arthur's pie?" Harry asked.

"Hmmm," said Jim, his mouth full.

"But..."

Jim swallowed. "He said I could have it. Wanna bite?"

"Shove it," said the disgruntled Harryoo.

"Heh heh," gurgled Jim climbing the stairs. "There's tea in the mess."

Linsey turned towards the ADO's office. Despite a lifetime dominated by men, it never ceased to amaze her, despite age, how child-like they remained.

24

Patricia Arnold was sitting at her kitchen table. Ben was in the garden kicking his ball against the wall that formed the row of garages at the back of their house. She had checked on him a while ago. His jeans and trainers were covered in mud and her lawn resembled a swamp. Despite this, she left him to it; he seemed to be enjoying himself and now with the housework finished, she could have five minutes to herself with a cheese toastie and the crossword. These few moments in a busy day were restorative. The tangy grilled cheese splattered with Worcestershire sauce was an emotional balm and the ciggy that followed was a friend that never let her down.

She scanned the lists for vertical and horizontal clues filling in the obvious answers. Three down, not solid, six letters, fifth letter 'o'. She leant over her plate as she took a bite.

"Hollow."

Did it fit the firewoman also? All mouth and no trousers. It had been what, over twenty-four hours since she contacted the station? The man there said she was on duty and would receive the message that afternoon. The usual emanation from authority that carried an empty ring.

She filled in the clue after confirming the second 'L' made nine across, language.

Her phone on the table next to her started to dance across the laminate while playing a space-age cadenza.

"Not now."

She picked it up, sighed, and hit the button.

"Hallo, Patricia, it's Linsey from the fire station. Sorry, I never phoned sooner, but I was out last night and busy this morning."

"Apologies accepted, I guess," came the abrupt response.

"Thanks for those kind words to my boss, and if in the future you think you need us, don't hesitate…"

"Sounds like you're giving me the bum's rush."
"What, no, I…"
"Changed your mind with the sisterly help."
Patricia's words cut to the bone.
"Pat. Can I call you, Pat?"
"'Course."
"All I've ever wanted to do is help. I'm new and naive and…"

Pat cut her short again, like a fish, hooked, she was determined to keep her on the line.

"I made contact because you didn't deserve my anger, although it was a bit creepy coming to my place of work, I know you genuinely wanted to reach out."

Patricia eyed the phone stuck to her ear and listened to the static, waiting for a reply. After five seconds that felt like thirty, she gave the fishing line a yank.

"You nosey bitch."

Did she hear a giggle or just a sigh? It was something more than static.

"Thanks, Pat. I mean it, if we can help, don't think twice."

"You can't help but I appreciate your concern, and for that, you deserve more."

"Well, as you say, nosey bitch, I'm all ears."

"Not like this. Ben has a birthday party to go to. I take him to his friends at five. Could you swing by then?"

"I'm working now, could be with you at six-twenty."

"Fine, I don't have to pick him up until seven-thirty."

"Ok."

Linsey and Patricia hung up simultaneously. Both women were happy that the discord had been resolved, and both wondered if they were doing the right thing.

25

The train started to move, breaking free from its inertia. A woman walking along the centre aisle towards the rear leant forward to counteract the train's thrust. In that instant, as he looked up, Eddie noticed her. It created an illusion of her walking up an incline. He looked out the window to restore his equilibrium. They were leaving Limehouse. He had showered at work, then popped home for an overnight bag. His afternoon had been spent on mundane tasks and three phone calls. It was the latter that occupied his thoughts on his journey up town.

First off, Ray.

His actions were out of character, drinking during the day. Eddie wondered if the fall had had more serious consequences than a broken wrist and whether or not he should talk to a doctor about his father.

Second, Charlotte.

She had got home without any delay and was enjoying the company of her family, especially her sister, whom she hadn't seen in over a year. She sounded slightly reserved and broke off mid-sentence to rebuke someone with a firm no. Eddie imagined her sister teasing her about her new boyfriend. It pleased him to think he may have been discussed and wasn't her dirty little secret. He played it as cool as he could, telling Charlotte to enjoy herself and call when convenient, but still hated her rather formal goodbye.

Third was Jane, to ask after Nev.

The train was easing itself into London past endless graffiti and an ugly mess of new, old, and very old buildings. Any attempt at a theme had long been abandoned. Youths were caged in a recreation area playing football. The authority's subliminal warning of longer periods of incarceration should they step out of line. Cars were stacked atop one another in a scrapyard, visible behind corrugated iron fencing topped off with barbed wire, then came a line of concrete bollards protecting a row of shops from potential ram raiders. Perhaps that was the theme, enclosure. People moved from one safe area to another. Although he couldn't imagine living in the East End, the sinister edge of his imagination created a shiver of excitement about the place.

He thought back to earlier this year and the conversation he had with big Nev. They had sat in Nev's garden and over a mug of tea (literally one mug, Nev refused to make Eddie a drink), he apologised for taking up so much of Jane's time and energy with his catharsis. His mother had died, and his father hardly spoke to him. Jane had helped him through it. She had been at his beck and call. He thanked Nev for his understanding, and now he would leave them alone. The one person he didn't thank was Jane. He could face the towering black belt, but when it came to her, when it came to facing her feelings, he couldn't. He phoned her shop, and she wouldn't accept his call. She deserved more. In the end, he had done the manly thing and run.

Nev, the good kind kind-hearted man, Nev the big, strong martial arts enthusiast, Nev the ever-patient husband, who loved his wife with a passion he could never articulate, was nobody's fool. The puppy love he and Jane had shared, however, lived inside them like refugees in love with a homeland to which they could never return. It was for them to let go of the past, for them to realise that any return to a once treasured place invariably reveals fault lines in the house of yesterday. Small cracks and fissures that time has covered with a smooth alabaster show through.

Nev accepted Eddie's gratitude and placed it alongside his own long-accepted understanding of their tripartite relationship. They were three people fighting a powerful common foe, love, and all they had was their thin cloak of virtue.

Eddie had wanted to stay close to them while knowing he shouldn't. Now a brain attack demanded he make contact. How could he not?

"Hallo, stranger."

"Hallo, Jane."

"How are you? You bumped into Charlotte."

Her monotone voice sounded like she'd been door-stepped by a politician she would never vote for.

"Yea, good to see her. How is he, Jane?"

"Ruined."

"Jane, I know Nev. He'll pull through, I'm sure. This won't ruin him."

"It already has, Eddie."

"How do you mean?"

Eddie heard a sharp intake of breath, keeping her emotions in check. "You know Nev, my Nev. He was never going to set the world alight, never the life and soul of the party. He was big, strong Nev, protector, provider. Mr reliable. All that." She paused.

"All that he had has been taken."

"Do you want to meet up for a coffee?"

"Oh, what and finish him off completely."

"You don't have to tell him."

"Oh, do me a favour, Eddie. I'm never gonna lie to this man again. I remember how hurt he was when I stayed late doing your hair and never telling him."

"Sorry, I'm an arse."

"Forget it."

"Is there anything I can do, Jane? If so, don't hesitate."

"No, thanks."

"Please give him my regards, Jane. My sincere regards for a speedy recovery."

"Will do. Charlotte said you are with someone. A Charlotte."

"Well, been on a couple of dates, that's all."

"Where did you meet?"

"In the National Gallery, Trafalgar Square."

"I know where the National Gallery is. Spreading your wings, eh. Plugged everyone in Estuary English?"

"Jane."

Eddie wanted to admonish her but under the circumstances, he knew he couldn't.

"Well, I hope it works out for you."

"Remember, Jane, anything, let me know."

Eddie hung up. Her pain was tangible, her anger with him obvious.

The train slowed to a stop at the end of the line. For Eddie, the turmoil he felt still had a way to travel.

26

Linsey pulled up outside her shared house. She couldn't go in, not yet. She needed to walk a while. Think about her conversation with Pat. She was angry with herself. Why didn't she listen to her bosses and walk away? The bliss of ignorance was lost to her now. Her life was darker, her emotions, what, unnerved, that at least.

The street was quiet. Parked cars were plastered in wet leaves. The inky sky, heavy with rain still to come, was suffused with burnt orange light pollution. As she passed one house, a large illuminated box bay window asking to be looked at displayed a group sitting at a table with drinks and cartons of delivered food. Laughter squeezed past the old wooden sash frames.

The chill night air urged her to return home.

Linsey zipped her fleece to the top. The warm collar and cosy pockets gave comfort.

She must remind herself of her feelings towards Pat when they first met. The desire she had to support her. She had pursued this woman, wishing to help. 'Well, be careful what you wish for, Linsey Rivers'. A phrase she remembered Sam saying to her when they were at training school together. She was hoping to get posted to Langdon, the county's busiest fire station.

"Why be careful?" She'd asked.

"I heard some of the watches are a bit rough and ready," he replied. Little did he know that was his destination, and she would get her wish by replacing him after his accident. She could do with more sage words from him now. The desire to confide in someone was strong, but who? Choosing the right person was like choosing a tattoo. Get it wrong and it's a mistake you're going to have to live with.

She had sat once again in that kitchen, but this time, Pat was doing the talking. She listened in rigid silence, unable to drink her tea as Pat described the abuse. The physical domination, casual slaps, a dig in the ribs, or hair pulled back hard with an arm wrenched up the back. That was ok. That wasn't every day, as long as he was in a good mood, as long as he was pleased. It was the mental coercive control that was constant. Even his absence, beginning with relief when he left, that brief hiatus before the day coloured like a darkening bruise. Looking at the clock as it ticked closer to his arrival, the sound of his key in the door.

She would have done everything to please him. The house would be spotless, the dinner ready, beers in the fridge. Then she would greet him and, in that instance, she would know. She knew that the slight possibility of a pleasant evening was gone. Dinner was taken in silence. The fear of dropping a knife and the scalding rebuke it would bring.

"Fuck sake, clumsy bitch."

His plate was left on the table, his mouth wiped with the tea towel before a few barbarous words.

"I'm going to the pub."

Then again, relief as the front door closed. She would clear away the crockery before resuming her vigil with the clock as it stole the time before his return. That was how Pat started. Linsey could remember her description verbatim. Pat's words were like insects caught in a spider's web, stuck, waiting for the horror to come.

It was clear to Linsey now. Pat's fear, her reluctance to open her door and engage in any way.

"He's a firefighter, isn't he?" Pat nodded.

Linsey, her throat dry, her tea untouched, asked the question to which she wasn't sure she wanted the answer.

"Does he work at Langden Fire Station?"

"I don't know where he works. He moved after she…" She paused. Saying it aloud opened the wound.

Linsey started to rock, ever so slightly, back and forth. She unzipped her jacket.

Pat looked across the table at the confused young woman sitting there. She lit a cigarette.

"My sister. It's her I'm telling you about. He killed her. Ben is her son, his…" She couldn't bring herself to finish the sentence.

Linsey didn't want to punish Pat further with questions that would cause further grief, but a bond had formed; they were united in their hatred of this incubus. This living nightmare of a man.

"How, Pat, how did he?"

Pat drew the smoke deep into her lungs.

"Your tea is getting cold."

Linsey took a sip. The bland flavour did little to calm the rawness she was feeling.

"Pushed her down the stairs."

"Wasn't he punished?"

"Couldn't prove it. He said she tripped and fell. Police believed him. When I say 'believed him,' they couldn't prove it."

She had sucked the cigarette down to the butt then, with absence of mind, stubbed it out.

"She would phone me from her bathroom, terrified, whispering in case he heard. On one occasion, I called the police. Worst thing I done. She wouldn't press charges and he came here, smashed the front door into my face and threatened to rape me if I interfered again. A female police officer attended the one call I made. She was disgusted enough to really push her colleagues not to dismiss the case so easily. She gave him as much trouble as she could, but ultimately, there was no proof, but I have proof. I know he killed her."

"How do you know, Pat?"

"Ben. I've had Ben since, it's a long story. The council house was in my sister's name, he had to get out. He said he couldn't take Ben. It was obvious he didn't want to. I took the boy. This beautiful boy, completely traumatised by what he saw and heard in his short life. You know he started hitting his mother, and now he lashes out. He gets upset or frustrated, like any kid does and his answer is violence. Then, it happened, one day in a complete tantrum, he threatened to push me down the stairs. I think, believe, he saw his father kill his mother."

"The other day, Pat, when he fell down the stairs, do you think?" Pat lit another cigarette.

"I've been too scared to think about it."

The car horn blasted Linsey from her trance. She stared into the headlights and, for an instant, thought she had been caught in wrongdoing. The glare slid past. She heard the faintest electronic whir as a window lowered.

"You alright, love?"

Linsey, now composed, nodded and gave a stupid thumbs up.

"We'll take care. I nearly hit you."

Linsey looked around to get her bearings, then turned for home. It wasn't that late, her flatmates were bound to be in still. She hoped they were in the kitchen having a drink while deciding on the night out. She would quickly change and join them. Tonight, she was going out again and, tonight, she was getting drunk.

27

Ray was hanging. He had woken from a profound sleep with a head and wrist vying for first place in the pain stakes. He had taken killers and his arm was feeling better but the whiskey wasn't letting him off that easily. There is retribution for the fun to be had from firewater, and the price to pay is more than the cost of the bottle.

"No sympathy, I'm afraid," said Eddie. "Self-inflicted wounds. Shot at dawn." He wanted to make light of the situation before he started in with 'the quiet word'.

He placed the sliced pizza on the table in front of his old man.

"Meat and two veg tomorrow, Dad. Can't live on this stuff."

Ray looked at the selection of colourful ingredients scattered across the doughy triangles with the expression of an archaeologist confronted with the Rosetta Stone.

"The Italians do."

"Ok, I concede."

Eddie took a mouthful; Ray nibbled.

"Ah ah ah, fer farck, that's hot. How's the wrist?"

"Getting there."

"Tablets work, got plenty?"

"Yep, phooo."

"Don't just blow it, eat it. Maybe not the best idea to mix them with alcohol, Dad."

"Look, Son, if you've come up to give me a bollocking, forget it. I'm not about to turn into an old soak."

"Not saying you are, but I've never known you drunk, ever. It worried me, and boy, did you sound drunk. Poor man's heroin, what was that all about?" Ray pushed his plate away.

"I ain't been right."

"Since when?"

"Since the move, really. Been more difficult than I imagined."

Ray couldn't hide his embarrassment.

Eddie sat back and took a mouthful of water, agitating it like a washing machine in his mouth.

I'm too young to get food stuck, he thought to himself.

"I keep a diary, Dad, have for many years now. I'm not in the same league as Tony Benn, just a few notes every day. It's surprising how a line or two can transport you back to another time."

Ray liked his son's verbose approach to the point he intended to make. It reminded him of Eve. His wife could be so long-winded that she would get lost along the way and never arrive at her intended destination. It drove him nuts. Now, he missed it.

Ray sat back and listened.

"Do you remember buying me a Letts diary for Christmas. I was eleven. I still have it. It's amazing how little my musings have changed over the years. West Ham lost again, that kind of thing. Anyway, I was flicking through an adult version recently, some entries reminding me of times with mum. Anyway, 20 January. Big mistake renting this place, like a prison cell, no character and freezing cold. Do you remember the flat I rented before buying in Leigh?"

Ray nodded.

"I'd been there a week when I wrote that. I lived there for a year, well, a little over, took longer than I thought to buy. Aren't you eating that?" Ray shook his head.

"Give it here. The entry on the day I left that flat could not have been more different. Enjoyed my time here, sorry to be leaving. Can you believe it?" Ray nodded.

"The point I'm making, Dad, is that moving is a big thing, takes time to adjust. This is a lovely flat and you've already made friends. Give it time and go easy on the poor man's heroin. Fancy a beer?"

"Obviously not, but I'll come with you, the walk will do me good."

"Good. I'll tidy up, clean me teeth, then we'll go. That mozzarella sticks to the pearlies like seaweed to a pier."

28

The watch gathered around the mess table. Harryoo was happy to be driving the ALP, and he had all night to work on Jim regarding tomorrow night. Adam and Perry were regurgitating their day. Arthur and Sean were deep in conversation; others read papers or looked at phones. Ken was in the kitchen singing along with the radio, "Take me to the moon, take me to the moon and zoom zoom zoom." Billy asked him if he wanted a hand with anything.

To all intents and purposes, a normal Sunday evening on the Red, waiting for what the locals had in store for them.

Linsey sat quietly with her tea, watching her colleagues, the people she placed her trust in. Whether it be a conversation with a scared woman or a building well alight, they had her back. When she was inside, these were the people on the outside looking after her. Good professionals, good guys. Trust can be a fickle companion, though easily undermined. A few words laced with doubt regarding someone's character, and the seed is planted. Patricia Arnold hadn't so much as planted a seed, but rather sowed a field in Linsey's mind. Pat was terrified of a man, and the fear had leached into her.

Now she sat at the mess table, telling herself that these men were good men. If only Pat had given her the name of her sister's killer, her tormentor. She had refused without justification. Linsey could only assume Pat didn't want her stirring up trouble within the service that would bring the villain back to her threshold.

Pat had told her of a time when things were good in her life, before Ben arrived. She would visit her sister. The three of them would sit and enjoy a beer in the garden. Laugh at life and their futures. A future that didn't include children, as far as he was concerned. Did Ben know, would he ever know that he was the reason for his father's hate, his mother's demise?

Linsey looked at Luke.

Her mate with a lovely wife and twin girls. The thought of him beating a woman was unthinkable. That knowledge helped with the perspective. She must convince herself that her biggest threat was her own imagination. She tuned into his conversation.

Luke was telling Eddie of a regular argument he was having with a neighbour.

"He fucking lights a fucking bonfire every fucking Sunday morning. Alice has to take the washing in. She gets the fucking ump. I get the fucking grief. Fucking drives me crazy."

"You've had a word I take it," said Eddie with his best concerned voice.

"A fucking word. I've asked him politely, very fucking politely, not fucking politely and…"

Luke ran out of politely's.

"Good fences make good neighbours," proffered Eddie. His only answer to a problem for which he had no answer.

"Try telling that to the plume of fucking shitty smoke," said an exasperated Luke.

She glanced around the room at all the guys. *They were great, weren't they?* Trust in your colleagues, that's all she could do.

Chris Everett came into the mess room and placed the saucepan on the table.

"Right, all the names are in there except Arthur's."

"We are drawing for the 25th and 26th, plus the 1st. So, the first six out. Arthur, would you do the honours?"

"Pleasure," said Arthur.

The days aforementioned were crucial days in the calendar. Everyone on the watch knew Christmas Day was the second day of their festive tour of duty this year, Boxing Day their first night, and New Year's Day would be the first day of the following tour. It had been a long-standing agreement amongst the watch that leave would not be booked in the conventional way over this period. So, six names, two for each day, would be pulled from the hat, or in this case, the saucepan and then a period of intense negotiation that included gentle persuasion, cajoling, and emotional pressure would usually commence.

Similar to a crisis at the United Nations Assembly, where members would listen to the debate in polite silence, then break up for urgent discussions about the best way forward. Alliances forged and broken. Beverages were taken in ante rooms where strategic plans were made. Urgent phone calls were made back home seeking approval of their actions from unforgiving pay masters. Finally, the winners must not appear to have won. The losers were congratulated on their magnanimity.

If only it were this straightforward on Red Watch Langden.

Christmas Day, especially for men with kids, and New Year's Day for those with a raging hangover, are the ones to bag. The night shift on Boxing Day after two days of festive eating, drinking, arguing, screaming kids, unlikeable relatives, and crap TV was considered by most a welcome break. The obverse also had to be considered. Money. All these days meant double bubble. Work them all and next month's pay packet would be a welcome boon. Finally, the partners. If the firefighters were the delegates at the assembly, the partners were the governments applying vicarious pressure. Diplomacy at home and at work was a high-wire act.

Billy Butler was first out.

Shoulders sagged. Chris wrote down his name. Billy was a single man with no children.

"You taking it?" Chris asked.

"Yep."

"Fuck sake," said Luke, married with twins.

"What?" Billy challenged.

"You ain't got any kids."

"Oh, so I'm to be punished for not having kids, eh?" Billy picked up the piece of paper bearing his name. "Would you like me to put it back in the pot?"

"Yes, mate."

Ken agreed, Chris's pen hovered ready to erase his name.

"I bet you fuckin would."

With that, Billy screwed up the piece of paper, popped it in his mouth, chewed then swallowed. His decision permanent.

Harryoo was next.

This rankled for different reasons. Harryoo's boy was a teenager and spent Christmas morning asleep and, weather permitting, the afternoon at the skate park.

The Christmas Day off was not a high priority for Harry. Nevertheless, he was pleased with the draw; it gave him leverage, especially with the dads of younger children. Harryoo liked driving the ALP, it never went out the doors as much as the two pumps. A Christmas Day could get him a few swapsies. He wouldn't be telling his Doreen. He'd sooner admit to shagging Flo, the cleaner, than be told by his wife that she expected him home carving the turkey.

"If you'd be so kind, Chris." Harryoo scribbled an air signature.

"One year, I'll come out the hat," said Ken.

Arthur had known Ken longer than most, and he had to admit to himself that he could never recall Ken being lucky.

"The day, this religious day, means so much to my Chimlin, and she wants to share it with me." Ken was going for the sympathy vote.

"I thought you told me Chimlin was Buddhist," said Adam.

"No, no, Catholic and devout."

"She's so devout that you married in a registry office," said Perry, a real practising Catholic.

"It was a Catholic one," replied Ken to general laughter that even he smilingly had to go along with.

Adam Martin and Jim Harris got Boxing night, and Perry Jackson couldn't wait to tell Rachel that he had New Year's Day off and she could go ahead with the party she was planning.

"So, last but not least," said Arthur, stirring the saucepan for the sixth name. "And it's Linsey."

"Fuck sake, the sprog; been here five minutes, shouldn't even be in the draw." Luke could not hide his exasperation.

"I don't want it," said Linsey.

"Now, now, Linsey love, don't be hasty; think about it. Think of all your options," said Ken, fighting till the end.

Ken was the only one she'd take a condescending 'love' from, but not his advice.

"Draw another, please, Guv. I don't want it."

Arthur stirred.

Eddie Hart, Chris Everett, Sean Stolly, Ken Taylor, and Luke Dunstford swirled and tumbled over one another in the saucepan, then came to rest. A thumb and forefinger plucked one of them from disappointment to happiness.

Arthur looked down the table and smiled. "It's Ken."

"Yess! Hee hee." He leant across to where Linsey was sitting and grabbed her wrist. "You done the right thing, Lins," he said shaking it.

"I suppose Chimlin's fucking Scottish now," mumbled Luke.

"Luke," Arthur spoke his name softly.

"Yes, Guv?"

"Make a brew, please."

"Yes, Guv."

Luke made his way to the kitchen while the winners considered their options.

29

Autumn was messing around. Cold snaps and warm days confounded logic. Parents argued with their children, insisting coats and jackets be worn while the kids pointed at the postie still in shorts.

"He will still be in shorts in January, now put that coat on."

Older folk booked holidays in winter sun now the urchins were back in school while others wondered how to pay for the summer holiday now a distant memory and where the cash for Christmas was coming from. Decorative tinsel and plastic paraphernalia with tenuous links to the Christian birth appeared in the shops. Exuberance and ennui bubbled and popped in equal measure as festive meals and piss-ups were being arranged in canteens and offices across the town. TV dramas returned.

Apples were being pressed for their tart alcoholic juice. Short eared owls hunted silently along the ditches. Marsh harriers strengthened by a diet of frogs, mammals and small birds readied themselves for the long journey to Africa. The weeks slipped by. Langden moved further from the sun.

Arthur Church opened the high window above his cot, then sat at his desk. It was six-thirty and in two and a half hours, another tour of duty would be complete. He liked to rise early and read. He could concentrate longer at this time of day. On this morning, he chose not to read but to think. Running a watch required an array of skills. Some were taught, others acquired with experience. The group dynamic of watch life must be considered and thought about; it was an aspect of the job he had rarely discussed with other officers. He knew it to be a weakness of his management.

More importantly, he needed to think about something that had been causing him some concern of late.

A clique on any watch could prove dangerous. In that situation, co-workers get detached and remote from one another. The antithesis of what firefighters require to be safe and effective. Arthur didn't think a clique had formed but he did notice a change in the climate.

Now a widower, he liked to volunteer at the local college where he assisted an English teacher in her class. The subject was English for Speakers of Other Languages. The college had provided Arthur with training. The lesson he had particularly enjoyed was about non-verbal communication. Seventy per cent plus of everyday communication is non-verbal. Therefore, it was not about what was said on the watch but more about what wasn't said.

Luke would never make an ambassador for women's rights but he and Linsey were thick as thieves. They sat next to one another at the mess and more often than not paired up to do the routines. It was like he was protecting her and, at times, when Luke was not around, she did seem a little subdued. Ken was increasingly a mother hen doing his best to keep everyone content with an array of food mainly designed for comfort eating and when he did offer an opinion, thought it carried weight. As much as he was loved by the watch, Arthur was not so sure. At the heart of the watch, Harry, Jim, Adam, Perry, and Billy were staunch in their attitudes to the job and everyone on the watch, guiding Linsey and supporting all the officers.

Though Arthur had never thought to ask why he transferred onto the watch, Sean appeared to fit in and his wealth of experience was a boon. Eddie was in the early throws of a romance which was consuming his thoughts. Arthur had to think hard to recall that feeling but knew it wouldn't be long before his right-hand man's feet touched back down on terra firma.

That left Chris. This quiet, charming, effective officer has a scab that he's been picking of late, thought Arthur, and despite a passage of time that would normally ameliorate the problem, he could see no sign of improvement. He liked to ask the members of his watch how they were but when the boss asks, it's problematic. Ok, walk into a room and ask collectively if everyone is alright, that's fine, no more than a greeting, but individually was different. Why was he asking? What had he seen or noticed? Did he have concerns on how well they were doing their jobs? It wasn't easy to intuit their terse responses.

So many times in his career, he had been approached by someone who had sidled up to him at an opportune moment to say, 'Have a word with so and so guv, he's struggling a bit at the mo'. Instigate it himself, ah, that was different.

So Chris and Linsey, only his imagination or something awry. Can't be work. Chris is too good an officer. If he had a problem with Linsey in that regard, he would address it head-on.

He needed to box clever. There is more than one way to heal a wound. There came a knock on the door that made him jump. Perry, not waiting for a response, walked in with a mug of tea.

"Morning, Guv, brew. Blimey cold in 'ere. Wanna shut that window? You'll catch ya death."

"Perry."

"Yes, Guv."

"You alright?"

"Yea, why? What 'ave I done?"

Arthur thought fast.

"You don't normally complain of the cold."

"Getting old, Guv."

The two men looked at one another.

Perry's tight-lipped smile and raised eyebrows were a non-verbal question which Arthur knew meant, 'Is there anything else?'.

"What's for breakfast?"

"Are you alright, Guv?"

"Yes, Perry. Why?"

"Ken has cooked exactly the same fry-up for years."

"Yea, you're right. You are not the only one getting older."

"Creeps up, Guv. Anyway, it's nearly ready."

With that, Perry walked out of the room, leaving Arthur with his tea and contemplation.

30

Eddie was doing circuits around Belton Woods. Reaching the top of Belton Way East for the third time, he was blowing hard. The nature reserve forms a scalene triangle of scrub and trees on a steep hillside. Steps from Marine Parade lead down to Leigh Railway Station. They dissect the woods and double as another form of torture for the fit or foolhardy attempting to run up them. Eddie turned to admire the estuary view. A flock of sparrows, a dozen say, rose from behind a hedgerow as if fired from a cannon; pigeons scattered without purpose, a bold fox considered the traffic. He would be pleased with another circuit, but he was more pleased when his phone rang. Unusually, he hadn't spoken to Charlotte today. It must be her; he was wrong.

"Ed."

"Hi, Jane."

"Can you come round now? It's Nev."

The front door opened as he walked up the path. He was met by Jane. She wore a large tee and baggy jeans; her hair was bed head. She wasn't crying, she was despairing.

He stepped inside.

"He's on the floor."

Eddie made immediately for the living room.

"No, no, upstairs, bedroom. I can't, I can't get anyone. He goes crazy if I mention the ambulance. Neighbours are at work, his mates are away walking. I can't get him up. I got no one to…"

Eddie stopped her. "We'll sort it," he said, his foot on the first step.

"Ed."

Jane placed a hand on his forearm.

"He is angry and aggressive."

Eddie looked at the hand he once held, walking home from school, the fingers that ran through his hair in her salon. The wedding ring.

"Guess he has a right to be, Jane."

Jane looked as if she had just been accused of a heinous crime.

"He's not angry with you, Jane. He's angry with the world. Come on, let's get him comfortable."

Linsey was in goal. It was three and in. Ben had scored twice but was reluctant to get his hat trick. He hated being a goalie. So did Linsey, so she hoped it wouldn't be much longer before Pat called them in for lunch. Over the previous few weeks, a loose friendship had formed between the two women. Like patients in a cancer ward, they shared a common malignancy. Pat's vetting of Linsey was complete. Linsey's motives were honourable and she was happy to welcome her into her home.

Linsey genuinely liked Pat and enjoyed swinging by for a cuppa, or in this case, a spot of lunch. If she was honest, really honest with herself, though, she did hope she could get Patricia to reveal the name of the man she feared. It was difficult to broach the subject without alerting Pat to her intention. Patricia had stopped talking about the anxiety she lived with, wanting only to create a happy home for Ben, unaware that the contagion now affected her new friend.

Linsey's desire to know the name had transmuted to a need. Her day-to-day life was being affected. Her male-dominated world dripped with innuendo, dark thoughts, and suspicion.

A once innocuous comment now carried an invidious barb. She had lived naively under the protection of her father, she loved, got on well with men she worked with, now, as if in a dream, the masked ball was over, as true identities were being revealed. Rapists, subjugators, domineering bullies. It was in their DNA, traced back to the cave. She had argued with her brothers when Mark had shown Howard a celebrity in his mag, followed by the comment, 'I would'.

Knocking the periodical from his hands, she had rounded on them both, accusing them of low and cheap sexism while they were in her and their mother's company. She was losing her focus. Her life, career, and relationships. It meant nothing to be aware of her fixation. Her mind was stuck on a Ferris wheel, and after every rotation, as she was ready to dismount, another round of unease began. A name would apply the brake to her turmoil.

Nev was sitting on the floor with his back against the bed. He, with the help of his wife, had got into this position. To get up onto the bed was beyond them both. The lift required muscle and two good arms. Nev had one, but the muscle wastage in it was significant.

"Hallo, Nev."

Nev snorted a wordless reply and looked at his wife with pure contempt. He pushed a word through his corrupted lips.

"Bich."

Eddie wasted no time with prevarication. He grabbed Nev under the arms and, from a squat position, lifted the patient. Jane quickly moved in, swinging his legs onto the bed. Eddie laid him back. Nev stared at the ceiling. A silence pervaded the room.

"I could murder a drink, Jane."

Jane looked at Eddie until the understanding of his request sank in.

"Of course."

Eddie stared at her. Jane nodded. Nev snorted. All knew their parts for the next act.

The two men listened to Jane reach the bottom step. Only then did Eddie pull the chair away from the vanity unit to the side of the bed and sit down. "Nev, what I'm about to say is not meant to mollify the anger you have. I can't begin to understand how you feel, but I do know how much you love that woman and how much she loves you. Your intelligence has not been diminished; force it to overcome this degradation and cut her some slack. You both need help. If you don't want me, fair enough, but you have to let her call on others or you will both end up in the hospital."

Jane came with a glass of water, eager to return to her husband's side. Eddie stood.

"Perfect, thanks."

He downed the glass in one.

Jane was keen to introduce some normalcy to the situation.

"Well, thanks, Ed. You've been a great help and we're sorry to have called on you. Aren't we, Nev?"

Eddie looked down at the stricken man. His reply was aimed at him.

"If you want my help, I'm here."

Nev's good arm elbowed into the mattress.

"I think he wants to sit up," said Jane.

"Here, let me."

Eddie placed the glass on the bedside cabinet, then grabbed Nev again under his arms and around his back, ready to hoist him to a semi-recumbent position.

Eddie heaved the leaden body and as he did so, Nev's good arm came around his neck. Nev pinned his mouth close to Eddie's ear. The two breaths were hot and wet on his skin, each carrying a whispered word.

Downstairs in the lounge, Eddie looked out at the overgrown garden.

"He'll sleep now," said Jane, placing the glass in the dishwasher.

"Would you like a coffee? I bought one of those Bialetti coffee pots you were always banging on about."

"If you don't mind, Jane, that would be great."

"Why would I mind?"

"Well, last time we spoke, I wasn't exactly flavour of the month."

"Have you wondered why?"

Jane never gave him a chance to reply.

"Your mother dies, a woman we both loved, you are in torment and Ray too, naturally, and I…"

"Jane."

"Shut up. I was there for you two all the way through your grieving process whenever I was wanted, there I was, and more, visiting the grave, placing flowers, taking Ray. Finding counselling for you. Then when you and your father kiss and make up and come out of your miserable fug, you both bugger off without a bye or leave. Thanks a bunch, Eddie. Hot or cold milk?"

"Cold."

He was scared to ask for hot. He was chastised.

"I'm sorry."

"Yea, so am I. Anyway, thanks for today, I appreciate it even if he doesn't."

"I'll always help, happily."

"That ain't happening, Ed, we both know that."

"But you need help, you can't carry on like this."

"I've asked Charlotte to come home for a day or two. I think he'll listen to her."

"Good luck."

"That's what I need, Ed, some good luck."

After the coffee, Jane walked him out.

Jane reached for the latch, but before opening the door, she looked up at the man she had loved all her life.

He returned her gaze with a shy smile, and in that moment, they could have been kids again outside the school gates, and he asking her out to a night at the youth club.

"What did he say when you helped him up on the bed?"

Eddie looked up the stairs to the closed bedroom door.

"Eddie, what did he say?"

Eddie returned her gaze.

"He said, you win."

Jane's laugh was rueful. She opened the door.

"He's there, ain't he?"

She tapped her temple.

"Inside, he's there and he's right."

"What do you mean?"

"You win, Ed. Look at you, your life now. You win, you always do."

31

Charlotte had had a busy time of it. The National Gallery, while welcoming the inquisitive scholar into its archive, needed to protect it like a mother protects her young. Did a budding historian seriously believe it acceptable to stick a post-it note on a valuable manuscript or handle rare photographs ungloved? Why did the fusty academic settle at a table with a delicate history laid in front of him, then delve into a scabby briefcase, not for a pencil and notepad but a sandwich in grease-proof paper, or worse, a packet of smokes? Didn't they read the instructions? Didn't they realise her man hadn't phoned? She could hand out acid-free slips, she could confiscate smuggled sustenance, but she couldn't phone Eddie.

Phone calls in the early days of a relationship warranted consideration. If she was the one who always made contact first, did she appear overeager? If she waited for him, would he think she didn't care? She knew it to be a negotiation that required compromise.

So today, she didn't make contact. She waited. He hadn't phoned. Why did she choose today to employ this strategy? Charlotte sat at her desk. It was covered in paperwork that was covered in marginalia. A tray of pens fought with paper clips, an eraser, and a small ball of coloured rubber bands. Buried beneath all her work was a stapler with her name tippexed on its black base. She knew it was there, somewhere. On the right-hand side sat the landline. If it rang, it was business, or her mother, who steadfastly refused a mobile.

"I'm at everyone's beck and call inside the house. I refuse to be when I'm out," she had informed her family. Her daughters nagged to no avail and her husband, the judge, while not agreeing with her, thought her argument carried weight.

In Charlotte's hand was her mobile.

Ring, dam you.

It rang.

"Morning, darling. Sorry, I haven't phoned; been one of those mornings. How are you?"

"Oh fine, been busy myself. Didn't realise the time. You ok?"

"All the better when talking to you."

"So, do tell what is one of those mornings."

"Oh, this and that."

He realised his evasion and corrected it.

"I was out running and Jane phoned. Her husband has had a stroke, remember, and had fallen. She needed help."

"She should have phoned for an ambulance."

"It's a long story, I won't bore you with it."

Bore or sidestep, she wondered.

"Anyway, this weekend. Can you come down? Chris, the leading hand on the watch, and his partner, Jamie, have invited us over for a meal. Chris likes to cook. His real name is Alec by the way, another long story, and I said I'd let them know today."

"Yes, that's fine."

Everything is just fine, she thought.

32

Persons reported means people are or maybe trapped inside a building on fire.

When a priority message containing that phrase came over the radio, it upped the ante.

In the rear cab of the water tender, Linsey and Jim immediately rigged in BA. Adam was driving, and Sean was in charge. They would arrive first. Time was of the essence. Smoke kills the majority of people who die in fires long before the flames attack the flesh; a few lungfuls and the brain is poisoned. No matter how familiar a room or home is to the occupant, once the carbon monoxide laced with cyanide and a deadly cocktail of other chemicals that reside inside a modern home start to burn, the mind becomes confused. The eyes see the door that leads to fresh air, but a bewildered brain cannot give the command. Death quickly ensues.

The lorry came to a stop outside the property. Smoke was issuing, but no sign of fire. Sean booked in attendance. Adam engaged the power takeoff from his driving position, then jumped out of the cab and went to the rear side locker that contained the hose reel. He released the brake from the drum and ran the hose reel to the front door before going to the rear of the appliance, from where he would pump operate.

The front door was wooden and half-glazed. Jim and Linsey stood to one side of it and put on their face masks. Linsey breathed in and sucked the mask to her face. She then reached behind and opened the cylinder valve that sat low on her back and drew her first breath of compressed air. She covered her hair and ears with a balaclava snood, then placed her helmet awkwardly on her head, struggling to secure it under her chin. Jim took her name tally from the harness on her chest and threw it with his on the floor near the threshold. This went against all they were taught about BA procedure but fuck it; if there were people inside, they didn't have a second to spare.

The house was in a paved precinct. The front door gave straight onto a common area. The fire appliance was only four metres away. The diesel engine roared, waiting to deliver water. The noise reverberated off the brickwork. Sean arrived with a small axe and, crouching to one side, tried the obvious but sometimes overlooked action of trying the handle on the front door to see if it opened. It didn't. Linsey could see Sean shouting instructions to Jim as he handed him the small axe. Linsey picked up the hose reel gun and saw her naked hands. *Fuck it, fuck it*, she fumbled inside her tunic. Thank Christ, they were there. Sean would crucify her if she had to ask for gloves.

She quickly put them on, pulling the elasticated tunic sleeves over them. She bent down again for the hose reel. Time slowed. Noise faded. Just her heavy mechanical breathing. If she closed her eyes, she could be on life support in intensive care, dreaming this whole scenario. Her mother's soothing voice saying her name over and over. Her brothers and their wives around the bed. Mark, Howard, and Michelle, concern etched on their faces; Nancy looking slightly peeved at all the attention she was receiving. Her father, where was he? She couldn't see him, but he was there. She could listen to his voice, 'Linsey, Linsey'. She looked up, not sure what would await her. It was Sean shouting at her. He glared through her visor.

"Linsey, I've been around the back, this is our way in."

"What?"

Did he ignore her, or not hear?

"When Jim breaks the glazing, be ready to hit any flame with a jet. Ok?" She nodded. All the noise returned, and her family faded. She knelt on one knee. Jim looked at her and nodded. She nodded back. He swung the axe at the corner of the glazing. It seemed counterintuitive not to hit the glass in the middle, but that is the toughest part. Hit the edges. The outer sheet fell away. He struck again and destroyed the double-glazed unit. There was no flashover, no flame. The smoke was lazy and reluctant to leave. Jim reached in and opened the door. She entered with him. The stairs were immediately to the right, but Jim made for the kitchen. He seemed confident with what he was dealing with.

Linsey pulled on the hose reel as it snagged on the newel post at the bottom of the stairs. The cylinder on her back hit a coat stand, which fell on her. She pushed it upright, doing her best not to get angry with the inanimate object. Inside her tunic, her tee shirt was soaked in sweat. The wet cotton chaffed her skin. Jim was moving quickly now. He had opened the back door and placed the shallow frying pan with its charred remains outside. Linsey looked at the blackened unit above the hob, its face cracked like a dried river bed. Jim came back from the living room and shouted, "Come on upstairs, leave the hose reel. Fire's out."

As he ascended the stairs, he punched the bleeping smoke detector off the ceiling. Jim found the unconscious teenager in the first bedroom. He grabbed him under the arms and made for the stairs.

"Carry on looking, Lins," he shouted as he descended.

Technically, a BA crew should never split up, but they had already broken the rules, one more wouldn't hurt, and no number had been put on that persons reported message. Alone on the landing, she watched the young lad's feet bounce down the stairs as Jim descended backwards holding the boy around the chest. So, this was it; all the training was now focused on the next few minutes. Since joining, she had been to mundane stuff, silly jobs, laughed at the absurd predicaments people get themselves into, and worked alongside the other agencies that provide emergency cover, but this is what the fire service does.

Search for bodies involved in the fire. She turned and went into the first bedroom. It was a typical teenager's room. Clothes strewn over a chair, a desk with a monitor, and a games console. On the wall by the bed, a hideous poster of the metal band Slipknot. High in the far corner, a long sooty strand of cobweb collected black carbon. She opened the window. The smoke was clearing; this would help. Beneath the bed was a rucksack and an empty half bottle of cheap vodka. The main bedroom was largely unscathed. The double bed made and the cot empty.

That left the box room. She was feeling more confident now. How long had it been since they booked in attendance? It could be four minutes or forty. Time had expanded, then contracted, pulled into a black hole with the gravity of the job. She was to learn later at the debrief that the initial phase had taken six minutes.

Making sure the fire was extinguished, securing the premises, and contacting the parents would take another hour.

As the features of the house became clear, so did the scenario of events. Parents out or away overnight had left their trustworthy son to his own devices. Boy, was he in trouble.

The box room was aptly named. It had room for a raised bed and a small desk. Clothes and toys were probably kept under the bed, hidden by the cabinet doors. The bed was unmade. Mum, in a hurry maybe, only had time for her own or… Her adrenaline spiked.

The teenager wasn't the only occupant. Her heart raced as she opened one of the doors below the bed. In the blackness, a small round face like the moon in a cloudless night sky gazed up at her. He pushed away from her trying for the darkest corner. She must have looked alien to him. If he could breathe, then so could she. She flung her helmet on the bed and ripped off her mask. She left the valve open as the compressed air filled the claustrophobic space.

"Come on, mate, you're safe now. So is your brother, but let's get outside and have some fresh air eh? What do ya say?"

Speaking to him without the BA set on made the little fella realise she was human and lovely like his mum. He reached up into her arms.

33

"When's Eddie back?"

"Next shift."

"Good. Every time I'm in charge of the water tender, it's the busy bus. I need a quite tour for a change."

Despite his complaints, Sean was in an ebullient mood and that went for the rest of his crew. He placed the tray of tea on the mess room table.

"Then again, I don't suppose we need him or anyone else really. Eh, team?" Adam, Linsey, and Jim concurred.

"Yep, rock up don BA, effect an entry, put the fire, and carry out two rescues," said Jim as he unwrapped his Mars Bar.

He took a bite before continuing.

"And where was the rescue pump all this time, Linsey?"

"Oh, still en route, I think, Jim."

"Or lost," added Adam.

"Fuck me, anyone think you never put out a fire before."

Adam mimed a fish being reeled in.

Perry gave a light shake of the head.

Harry and Ken were looking in Parker's guide and discussing car prices.

Luke couldn't resist taking the bait while being a little jealous of Linsey. He had yet to carry out a rescue from a fire.

"Anyway, I thought you said the fire was out."

"Technically, it was but we weren't to know that as we rushed in with…" He hesitated.

"With scant regard for ourselves," suggested Linsey.

Jim had many qualities as a man and skills as a firefighter but eloquence was not to be found in his tool box.

"Yea, with scant regard for ourselves."

"Can't listen to this shit."

With that, Luke got up and took his tea with him.

The water tender crew looked at one another and enjoyed their mutual success.

Arthur and Chris walked in.

"Who has upset Luke?" Arthur asked.

"His bosom buddy," said Perry.

"Linsey!"

Arthur effected a comedic rebuke.

Linsey suddenly felt embarrassed about the boast. She coloured.

"I'll go and have a word with him, Guv."

"No, no, you stay put. If he can't take it, he shouldn't have joined. Just remember, Linsey, pride comes before a fall."

"Yea, remember that," said Jim.

"Never had you for a piss taker, Lins," said Adam.

"It's the way of the modern recruit," concluded Sean.

Linsey took a swig of her tea while considering her repost.

"Bastards."

Ken looked up from his mag.

"Linsey, not very ladylike."

Harryoo tutted.

It was like growing up with her brothers. Through the days of innocence, not understanding their cruelty to a time of culpability and love.

"What you two looking for, mobility scooters?"

An appreciative ripple of laughter swirled around the table.

"Ok, well done, the pump's crew for a sterling job."

Arthur took charge.

"If I had given Perry the right directions, we would have been there sooner, but all's well that ends well. Anyway, I've been on the blower with SHQ, spoke to Leo Grant about the latest training packages, including anything on the appropriate behaviour on watches of mixed sex."

"Good," said Harryoo. "The way we've just been spoken to, I think Linsey needs it."

There was a gentle House of Commons murmur of approval.

"Seriously, boss, do we need it?" Sean interjected.

"We're fine, ain't we?"

"Fine we may be, Sean, but it's known as covering one's backside. If I have to take the likes of those two Herberts," Arthur pointed at Ken and Harryoo, "to task, then they can't plead ignorance."

Ken and Harryoo did their best to look hurt.

"Guv, do they have any training packages for officers on topography?" Harry asked.

"Touché," replied the smiling station officer.

"Now, how about mopping the bay before we go home?"

The mugs were placed on the aluminium tray, chairs were left at argumentative angles, and Harry stuck the Parkers in his back pocket. Linsey took the tray into the kitchen and started to load the dishwasher. She was followed in by Sean.

"Linsey."

"Oh, you made me jump."

"Sorry, Linsey. I just wanted to say how well you done today. I know I've given you a hard time of late, but I hope you realise it was for a reason, and today I think we saw its fruition. Well done."

She waited for the sting in the tail. Thought about asking Sean to repeat the comment, but decided on a simple thank you.

Sean smiled and walked out of the kitchen, leaving her to her thoughts.

34

"What on earth is that?"

Jamie and Chris were staring at the yellow splats of cheese dolloped across the baking sheet. Chris studied his culinary experiment like a scientist, thinking back over the sequence of events and searching for a missing link.

Jamie wore his expression, usually saved for people with no colour coordination.

"They are supposed to be parmesan thins. To go with the minestrone."

"Well, they look like something I scrape off the windscreen, dearheart. Go with the breadsticks, can't go wrong with breadsticks. Is the wine breathing?"

"Yep."

The doorbell rang.

Jamie greeted Charlotte and Eddie with his natural bonhomie. He kissed Charlotte on both cheeks.

Eddie hated this bit. He just wanted to hand over the bottle and the flowers and shake hands, maybe.

Jamie eased the coat off Charlotte's back, clocking the label as he hung it up. "Your turn." He looked at Eddie.

Eddie gave a startled jump like a dullard when told to join in.

He held out his hands.

"I'll take those," said Charlotte.

Eddie thrust the gifts into her hands, shucked off his jacket, and passed it to his host.

Jamie didn't check the label this time.

Chris and Jamie's house was old, high-ceilinged, with elegant, spacious rooms. The one downside was the narrow entrance hall. Furniture had to come in via the garden patio doors. It also meant Eddie couldn't get past Jamie without a degree of rudeness. He was trapped.

"So, are you going to kiss me?"

"Er..."

"Oh, if you have to think about it, don't bother. Go on in, your subordinate is in the kitchen fretting over his Osso buco." Eddie squeezed past Jamie and Charlotte.

"I love teasing him. Come on, I'll show you the house. You look gorgeous by the way."

"Christ, that's hot. I wish I knew my way around an Indian menu." Linsey was meeting her sister-in-law, Michelle, in the local curry house for three reasons. She liked Michelle, she valued her opinion, and for some inexplicable reason, she fancied a curry.

"Just ask the waiter, they will tell you the mild ones. Don't you think Indian waiters are the politest? Always happy and polite."

"That would be too easy," replied Linsey to Michelle's suggestion. "Come to think of it, yea, they are."

"How's work?"

That is the fourth reason, thought Linsey. *Michelle is intuitive as fuck.*

Linsey swigged her Cobra.

"How do you know I want to talk about work?"

"Well, you ain't pregnant."

"How do you know?"

"How does any woman know? Anyway, you love where you live, all's well with mum and dad, and as far as I know, you ain't bitch slapped Nancy. So work." Michelle snapped a poppadom.

"I do like to see you, Miche."

"Likewise, leaving the baby with Howard for an hour is heaven, but you could have come to the house. Even your brother remarked on it when I told him where I was going."

"I didn't realise I was that obvious."

"It's not a bad trait, Lins, openness. Is it the misogynist? Giving you a hard time?"

Linsey watched her sister-in-law tuck into her creamy korma. Choosing a confidante can be fraught, but Michelle was a safe bet.

"Well, that's just it, Miche, he has been the exact opposite. Friendly and polite even when we are alone, and to top it all, praise. A good old fashioned well done with knobs on."

"Really?"

"Yea, done a good job, know I've been hard on you but it's part of the training, etc., etc."

"When did he start being nice to you?"

"Er, a few days ago."

"Could you pinpoint it exactly?"

Linsey separated some rice from the red-hot sauce.

"Well, it was early evening. I was in the mess room with my books out studying, everyone else except Sean was playing volley. I knew he was in the watch room doing paperwork. He comes into the mess wanting a cuppa. Now that night, I was the duty bod, so tea making, helping with the dinner, etc., was my job. I jump up straight away to make him one. 'No, no, Lins', he says, 'stay there, I'll do it. Want one?' He brings me a drink, sits down, and asks me about my day and other stuff."

"Waiter," called Michelle.

A young, skinny man in a white shirt, black waistcoat, black trousers, and matching trainers attended their table.

"Could we have a small dish of yoghurt, please?"

Linsey ate some rice.

"So, he has been a complete arsehole since he joined the watch and just like that, he changes?"

"Yea, I guess so."

"Leopards don't change their spots, Lins. Be wary, I'd say."

The waiter returned with Michelle's order.

"There we go, Lins, mix that in your ruby. It'll take the edge off."

"This wine is delicious. Is that the bottle we brought?" Eddie asked.

"Don't be silly, darling, one doesn't serve cooking wine with Osso buco." Jamie's acerbic wit was the perfect accompaniment to an intimate meal with friends.

Eddie watched Charlotte hide her giggle behind the flat of her hand. He loved the cute affectation.

"It's a Barolo," said Chris.

"Have you enjoyed cooking for long, Chris?" Charlotte asked.

"A couple of years now. It's not like this all the time, though. When Jamie is flying, beans on toast is normally top of the menu."

"Any particular reason?" Eddie asked.

"Intrigue. The telly is inundated with cooking. Jamie would be in some far-flung corner of the globe, and I'd be watching them with the TV dinner on my lap, wondering what all these elaborate dishes actually tasted like, so I bought a recipe book and started."

Chris pointed behind him at the bookshelves full of Jamie's crime thrillers and his culinary library.

"Cooking and crime," said Charlotte.

"The crime is Jamie's."

"I love a bit of blood and gore. More wine?"

"You should do a meal for the watch one night; they would love it."

"Yea, stand there in my pinny fussing over the oven and whisking egg white. That's never happening."

The hard edge to Chris' comment left no doubt that something was awry.

"Chris, they would love it if you cooked."

"Yea, most of them. Anyway, let's have your plates. You wait and see what I've got for dessert."

Chris collected the plates and disappeared into the kitchen.

Charlotte reached for Eddie's hand that rested on the table.

His mouth smiled, his eyes didn't.

"You have a lovely house, Jamie."

"Thank you, Charlotte."

"It's not dissimilar to yours, Charlotte," said Eddie. "Same age, I reckon."

"Solid Victorian stock," said Jamie, sipping.

"Not going anywhere."

"Well, the inexorable slide down the hill seaward hasn't begun yet."

Jamie wiped the corners of his mouth with the white linen napkin, eased his chair away from the table, and crossed his legs.

"Did Alec mention we had a new water main laid into the property last year?" Jamie never called his partner by his ubiquitous nickname.

"Come to think of it, yea."

"I was home at the time, so amused myself watching the muscled forearms. Don't you find a strong arm attractive, Charlotte, dig their way across that pathetic expanse Alec refers to as the front garden? When the trench reached the house, they discovered the property just sits on the earth, no foundation at all, and this recent extension we are in now sits on six feet of concrete."

"Guess they knew what they were doing," said Eddie.

"Who the Victorians or the new Elizabethans? Anyhow, it's surprising what a little digging can expose, Eddie," said Jamie pointedly.

"There we are."

Chris stepped between Charlotte and Eddie, placing their desserts in front of them.

Jamie looked on. His partner of ten years wore a child-like expression as he served, like a young innocent home from school, eager to show what he had made. He pulled the chair up to the table, ready for his dessert, then drank deep from his water glass, hoping to cool the emotional ache in his throat. "Creme brule with a raspberry coulis and macaroons."

"Please, don't tell me you made the macaroons," cooed Charlotte.

"I have a friend called Waitrose."

"No, biscuits are not his forte. Tell them about your parmesan thins, darling." Chris laughed.

"Do you want dessert?"

"Darling, I'm positively salivating."

"Well then, zip it."

Chris stepped back into the kitchen.

"Well, thins?" Charlotte asked.

"No, no, I'd never betray him. He will tell you and then I'll tell you who we had on my last flight."

"Ooh, I'm all ears. Ed, wait till Chris returns."

Eddie refrained from cracking the sugar glaze. *My first rebuke*, he thought. He watched rather than listened as Jamie and Charlotte engaged in a conversation about the large Mapplethorpe photographic print easily admired from where they all sat.

Alone, he surveyed the scene of domestic bliss. The white table cloth, candles, the faintest strains of Billie Holiday from the Bose speakers, an array of white orchids and Swedish glass. Carefully placed scatter cushions and an elaborate screen that probably hid nothing more than an unsightly wall socket. It made his flat seem like a cell. He had a sudden urge to leave, to get up and walk out of the house. The evening suddenly demanded too much of him. It demanded emotion; it spoke of contentment and shared purpose. He imagined walking across the room, picking up the azure Scandinavian vase, and dropping it on the parquet floor. He had read a poem recently. The final couplet ran across his mind:

It's just a life of barbs and riches.

Navigating the razor wire and kisses.

The razor wire that he had tried to avoid earlier that evening. Charlotte's interrogation of his visit to Jane and Nev's. She didn't seem to accept that he was the only available help, and he was not going there again anytime soon. It was obvious that the avoidance of her questions irritated her. He had kissed her long and hard, explained again the long-standing friendship and the duty that it brought with it. Was she placated? He hoped so.

Chris sat back down and looked around the table.

"I hope you enjoy it."

"Looks delicious," said Charlotte. "Now, about these parmesan thins."

Linsey made her way home. The yoghurt had cooled her dinner, but her mind was still in a fever. Michelle had provided good counsel even with her own take on the Machiavellian saying, "Keep your friends close and your enemies close enough to kick in the balls."

Sean's actions were, the more she thought about it, out of character. If it were a choice between his former or latter behaviour, though, she knew what she would plump for every time.

She turned the heating up in her car and adjusted the settings to blow warm air over the windscreen and her feet. She thought about driving to see Pat. It had been a while since she had heard from her, but it was getting late for social calls. Her mind drifted back over the rescues from the house fire. They had been told that both boys were fine. The elder one was being kept in overnight for observation, so he had another twenty-four hours reprieve before his father killed him.

She wondered how the little fella would be returning to the place that had always provided his ultimate security and now had turned on him. No matter how high and solid the castle walls, their irrelevant when the fiery dragon is locked in with you.

Linsey pulled onto her driveway. The living room light was on, but no one had thought to draw the curtains. She got out, looked at the lawn cast in a yellow light, and thought it could do with one last cut before winter.

35

When a firefighter books late travelling, it means he or she has made a phone call to the station to say they would not be on time for work. Usually, it is ten minutes stuck in traffic. Jim was nearly an hour late. The Red sat around the mess table, enjoying each other's company. The lorries hadn't turned a wheel all day and the older hands hoped for an equally quiet night.

Jim was never late without good reason, so the watch got to pondering what explanation would be forthcoming. This meant a second round of tea as they waited and cogitated.

"Car broke down."

"Jim's cars don't break down."

"How did he sound on the phone?"

"How'd ya mean?"

"You know normal, fucked off."

"Hard to tell."

"I know he is looking after his dad's boxer while his parents are on holiday."

"Fucking 'ell, two boxers in one house."

"That's the Harris family, love their dogs."

"Perhaps, it got out."

Jim walked in. He said good evening and sat at the table.

Adam passed him a mug from the freshly made second pot.

"Thanks, Adam. Sorry, I'm late, Guv."

"Come on, we want more than that," said Ken. "You do realise how long we've had to sit here."

"You ok, Jim?" Linsey asked.

As much as she liked going out the doors, if the bells went down now, she'd curse. She had a feeling about this one.

Jim, the happiest and go luckiest member of the watch, appeared perturbed. The silence around the table had an air of foreboding. Surely, it could not be too serious or he wouldn't be here was the undeclared consensus.

Yea, this is going to be good, they all thought.

Jim started.

"I'm looking after my dad's dog this week."

"There, are told ya."

"Shut up."

"Emma was having her hair done. The hairdresser had just arrived and was setting up when she said dad's dog hadn't been out."

"Why only your dad's?"

"My boy had taken ours earlier, but I won't let him take both, too much for him. So, I thought I've got time. I grab the lead and out we go. I take him round his favourite route and then bump into a neighbour I ain't spoke to for a while. 'Got to go, mate', I said, 'or I'll be late for work'."

Jim looked at his mug of tea, but he wasn't really looking at it; he was steadying himself for what he was about to say.

They leant in.

"I get back to the house and as I look down into the kitchen…"

"Down?"

"Fa fuck sake, shut up."

"Yea, sloping site, the pavement is raised outside our place. So, I look in the window and there is Emma sitting on a chair looking at a mag with some cape wrapped round her and all these bits of tin foil hanging in her hair. As I go past the living room window, I look in again to see the fuckin hairdresser sitting on a dining room chair with…" Jim paused.

The scene around the mess table resembled a 3D photograph. No one moved, no one blinked; breathing was imperceptible.

"With his cock out and my dog licking it."

Linsey looked down at the table. She was squeezing her mug so tightly to suppress her laughter, she thought it might shatter in her hands. A slight 'huhem' escaped.

No one noticed.

"What did you do?"

"You haven't, you know?"

"What?"

"Killed him."

"You are one stupid cunt."

Jim took up where he had left off.

"I couldn't go in and confront him."

"Because?"

"Gemma's hair."

"Good point."

"Fuck Gemma's hair."

Jim refrained from commenting.

"Then what?"

"I waited outside the house until he came out. I grabbed him by the garden gate."

"Painful."

No one laughed.

"I slapped him."

"Slapped him!"

"Yea, hard, side of his head. Told him never to darken my door again."

They leant back.

This needed some time to consider. Each man had to think about Jim's response to the situation, and their own response had they been confronted with the same thing, or was it a load of old bollocks and the best late travelling story ever.

Linsey could tell. Jim's features always struggled to hide glee when he was messing around. It was his eyes; they would be wider, eyebrows slightly raised. Tonight, they were clouded with a cataract of concern. For his wife, whom he adored, for allowing this man in his home, and for the abuse to his dog, whom he loved.

She broke the silence.

"The kids, Jim?"

"Out with their other grandparents, thank Christ."

Arthur looked at Eddie.

Eddie nodded.

One of them would just check on him a bit later.

Ken sighed. "I thought I'd heard everything. Right, I've got to get dinner started."

A flurry of action took place, mugs chinked, chairs complained; only Billy Butler remained seated, still considering Jim's plight.

"How was Emma?" He asked.

"How do you think she was?"

"I mean, was she disappointed?"

"Disappointed?"

"Yea, you know, the bloke preferring the dog."

Everyone waited for Jim to laugh before they joined in.

36

The caravan was gone before they got there. Dumped by the side of the dual carriageway a few days earlier, it was only a matter of time before person or persons unknown decided to light up the night sky.

The rescue pump and water tender attended the incident. The two appliances took up the fend-off position. It closed the near side lane but allowed general traffic to ease past in the offside lane.

Eddie grabbed Linsey by both shoulders.

"Do not under any circumstances go to the offside of the lorries for anything. Understand?"

"Yes, Eddie."

Linsey knew what had happened to Sam, Eddie's last recruit. He went onto the outside of the fire engine, stepping into the live lane at the same time as a motorcyclist came through. It had cost him his career and nearly his life.

Luke kicked and picked at the burnt detritus.

"What you looking for, Puke?"

"Don't know, Lazy, but you never know, do ya."

Linsey shook her head. She wasn't sure if she knew or not.

The ALP was passing; it had been to fire alarms actuating in Grays. It slowed, and Sean lowered his window to shout some general abuse. Harryoo was about to hit him with the hose reel jet when Arthur shouted a no.

"The other road users, Harry."

"You're right, Guv. It was Perry, he told me to do it."

Chris came from around the back of the caravan as Sean drew level.

"Chris, Chrissy."

"Yea."

"You trod in something. Look at your heel, left one."

Chris lifted his heel and looked over his shoulder.

"Ooh ducky, get you," Sean shouted out, then laughing, closed his window as they drove off.

Linsey witnessed the scene.

"Alright?"

"Yea, just annoyed at myself by being caught out by…"

Chris didn't complete the sentence.

"Not what was said but who said it, yea."

Chris knew Linsey was whip smart but didn't feel confiding in her was the correct thing to do.

"It doesn't matter, Lins."

Linsey knew it did.

"Can I speak freely, Chris, Alec?"

"I don't mind the nickname. It's meant with good heart."

"By the majority, yea, and that's where we have something in common." Chris looked past her to the rest of the crew putting away the equipment and preparing to leave.

"Are you telling me you're gay?"

"No, I'm not. I'm saying you and I are in the minority, and minorities are easy targets for bigots and bullies. Maybe it's time to call him out."

"No, the rest of the watch like him."

"We think they do, but we don't know and he is careful; he chooses his time and place to let the bile drip from his mouth."

"Well, I ain't doing anything official, Lins. I can fight my own corner and I will choose my time and place. You, on the other hand, can come to me or Arthur and Eddie at any time you feel unhappy."

"Oh, so what's good for the goose is not for the gander, eh? I can fight too, but we can't keep letting him get away with it, Alec."

"You're right, Linsey, let's think on, yea. Don't call me Alec; at work, I'm Chris, ok."

"Alright, don't throw a hissy fit."

Arthur was standing next to the lorry as Harryoo wound the hose reel back into its locker.

"Are those two fighting?"

Harry looked up. Chris and Linsey were on the grass verge, a large expanse of wasteland behind them. Chris had his arm around her neck, ruffling her hair; she had both arms around a leg, trying to pull him over.

"Yes, Guv, I'd say they're fighting."

"Hmm… Well, before you put that away completely, give a little squirt in their direction."

"My pleasure, Guv."

37

Linsey left work sharp at nine. She had a busy day in front of her; that grass wasn't going to cut itself, but first, she was going to Pat's supermarket. It was one of her days at work, she just wanted to pop in and say, 'Hello, is everything ok?'. She had tried to contact her again last night to no avail. It worried her that her calls were not being returned. Apart from her friend's silence, she felt ebullient. Sean was still being nice to her and the talk she had with Chris gave her confidence going forward.

She got out of her car and walked briskly, head down. The reluctant pale rain was light enough to be swirled on the breeze, delaying its final destination. The shop was quiet. The manager stood admiring his Christmas display. "Excuse me, I'm looking for Patricia Arnold. I won't keep her long, just a quick message."

"Patricia is not at work this week."

"Oh, holiday," surmised Linsey.

"Sick."

"No! What's wrong?"

"Not at liberty to say I'm afraid, sorry."

Linsey had rapped on the door three times to no avail. She now maintained a regular tattoo on the knuckle of her forefinger. If Pat was ill, she had to be at home. She had nowhere else to go. Ben would be in school, more than likely taken by Bren.

Linsey was about to go around the back when she heard the safety chain slide across. The door opened enough for the words to escape.

"Go away."

"Pat, it's me, Linsey. What's wrong?"

"Please go away."

Linsey thought of making a joke, 'why you caught leprosy?', before instantly discarding the workplace dialogue as inappropriate. Pat's voice was ladened with fear not disease. Instead, she returned the plea.

"Please, Pat, let me in. I'm worried about you and Ben."

She stood at the door waiting for a reply. Her mind went back to their first meeting. The door ajar, hiding a frightened woman.

"Pat, I can't possibly leave. I can tell you are worried, scared, and that scares me, Pat. Can we talk, Pat? Face to face. Help one another. Pat, please let me in."

"Are you alone?"

"Of course, Pat. I'm not at work. I went to the shop thinking you'd be there cos you ain't been returning my calls, Pat. The manager said you were off, sick. I came straight round to see what I could do."

The acrid tang of cigarette smoke assaulted Linsey's nostrils, and with it, a fear slowly rising, causing a dull ache in her throat. The tar-ladened fug stimulated Linsey's brain and chilled her as thoughts ordered themselves in a way she hoped was wrong. There was one person who created this alarm in Pat, one person who worked in the fire service. Had he returned, and what for, his son? What other reason could there be? What other link?

No, she thought, *please no*.

"Pat, please let me in. I'm scared, Pat, for both of us."

Linsey turned and looked along the street. It was quiet. No passers-by, parked cars empty, a distant hammering the only nod to human life. She felt cold.

The chain slid back, and the door opened. She stepped inside.

When Eddie got to the front of the queue, he still hadn't made his mind up about the blueberry muffin.

"Alright," asked the girl behind the counter.

"Yea, can I have a small cappuccino with no chocolate, please?"

"To have in?"

"Yes, please."

"Anything else?"

"Er no," he said, handing over his money.

"Was that a small cappuccino?"

"Yes, please."

The ground coffee was compressed into the portafilter and attached to the group head.

"Is that to go?"

"No, have in please."

The frothed milk was layered over the coffee.

"Chocolate?"

"No, thank you."

The Italians say you eat a cappuccino but never with chocolate, thought Eddie. He also wondered if the barista listened to a word he said. He found an empty table, knocked the previous occupier's crumbs off the chair seat, and sat down.

He got his phone out and checked it for messages, then placed it on the table next to his cup. He could phone his father to see how he was doing, but would be given short shrift. He could phone Charlotte, but she would be busy at work, and they were calls he didn't really want to make. He wanted an incoming.

He wanted Jane to phone and ask for his help again. He wanted to know how Nev was doing, if he had improved, but first and foremost, he wanted to see Jane. He felt terrible about how he had treated her. After he had resolved his differences with his father and got his work-life balance back in order, an order Jane had done so much to help with, he had gone and seen Nev and told him how he would leave them alone, not her. She deserved more, and her recent rebuke stung. Thinking about it now, he realised the remorse he felt was compounded because he had to be told, not realising it himself. How selfish was he?

He wanted to walk into her shop late evening when all the customers had gone. He wanted to sit in the chair and, while she snipped and ran her fingers through his hair, tell her about his day. Tell her about Linsey and how well she fitted in. Tell her about the new leading hand Sean, and of course, his dad; she would definitely want to know about Ray. Maybe even visit him in his new home.

He drank the lukewarm coffee and spooned some foamy milk into his mouth.

Most of all, he just wanted to see her. He could drive by her house. He used to cycle past her house as a kid on the off chance of seeing her. Why not now?

'Oh hi, Jane. I was just passing through' and if she said 'Well, keep passing through', it would be hard to bear. He looked through the shop window with its fake Christmas frosting in the corners. A strong wind was driving down the temperature. An old man stood at the bus stop holding his hat by its broad rim. The Jack Russell shivered at his feet. Broadway was always busy. A car double-parked, waiting for another to pull out from the parking space. The supermarket door opened and closed with every passerby. A woman behind him laughed. It was deep and sexy. He wanted to turn and see what she looked like.

He had chosen a life on the periphery, and it suited him that way, but nevertheless, he had to admit sometimes it was lonely.

Pat and Linsey stood behind the closed door, staring at one another. Was it pain or fear Linsey saw in her friend's eyes? She moved to embrace her. Pat stepped back and, feeling the wall behind her, sank slowly to the ground. She hugged her knees. Linsey went to the kitchen and returned with an ashtray.

"Here."

She then sat on the stairs and waited for Pat to speak and the tension in her chest to ease.

"I phoned the station."

As Pat spoke, Linsey felt lightheaded. She knew what was coming. It was obvious now. She felt sickened by her ineptitude. The questions she could have asked, enquiries made, people she could have spoken to.

'Don't get involved, Linsey', but she did, and now this lovely woman was paying the consequences.

"And?" She asked.

Pat stubbed out her fag.

"I asked for you. 'Who shall I say is calling?' he said. I told him and, in that split second, recognised his voice. There was a silence, ten seconds perhaps, then he said you weren't at work and put the phone down."

"Ok, Pat. I'll deal with it."

"Deal with it. You! Look how you have dealt with it."

"I'll, I'll go to my superiors, Pat. I'll tell them."

"Huh! Do you think they care? They didn't care last time. He's been here, the same night."

"Pat."

"In this hallway with his hand on my throat, he told me never to contact the station again; never to say anything to anyone, or he would make my life a living hell. My life. He didn't even consider Ben's. His own son, who stood watching from the kitchen door."

She lit another cigarette and got up from the floor. For the first time since letting Linsey in, she looked her in the eye.

"Next job you get and your bleeding heart wants to do some good for the poor wretch, think twice, then walk away. Now, if you don't mind, get out." As she walked to her car, her vision blurred by tears, Linsey tripped on an uneven paver and fell on her hands and knees. A tear fell and spread across the stone like ink on blotting paper. No one came to her aid. She got up and, in her foolishness, limped to her vehicle. Once inside, she held her aching knee and sobbed.

Charlotte stopped for lunch and decided to pop out to the crypt in St Martins for a what, hmm, soup, yea hot bowl of soup with bread that had thick crusts, good for soaking up the creamy broth.

She sat at a table near the wall and got out her book, tested the soup for seasoning, and then looked as she knew she would across to the table where she had sat with Eddie the day they met. It was littered with leftovers for someone else to deal with. Obviously, the recent occupants were too busy or ignorant to bother.

Charlotte hunched over her food and, with her left hand, held open her book. She started to read, her eyes scanning the words, but her mind was elsewhere. Had she and Eddie moved on, progressed in the smallest way since that day at that table? She had worried more than once about bearing her heart to him too soon, but she wanted no skeletons, a clean slate. The doubt that dominated her thoughts was of Eddie's honesty. One did not need feminine intuition to detect the problem. It was plain. Eddie Hart was an open book regarding every aspect of his life bar one, Jane. When she was mentioned, his hand covered the page like a schoolboy scared that his juvenile scribblings of love might be seen by the teacher walking the aisles.

Jane was married, had a family, but Charlotte knew that was not a barrier to feelings. She should ask him directly about this, but then the frightening spectre of choice appears. She had been on the wrong side of a man's choice and it was desolate. So, let it hang. It was still early in the relationship, cut the paranoia, and enjoy one's lunch. She looked back over at the table. It had been cleared and cleaned of its sad misgivings.

38

Since joining the fire service, Linsey had known trepidation, fear even. The first day at training school, the first fire, the first day on station, but everything she had learnt so far had not prepared her for this. She walked across the yard looking for his car, hoping he would not be on duty this day. Leaves the colour of mud were stuck on the cold concrete and a couple of windscreens, a seagull that couldn't sing let out a sore-throated ululation from its perch on the TV aerial. Her knee was bruised from her fall. The dull ache reminded her of the visit to Pat's and the scolding she received.

"Next time your bleeding heart wants to do good."

Christ, that hurt so much. She remembered running in from school as a kid and telling her father the name-calling she had been on the receiving end of during play.

Sitting her on his lap, he would say to her, "Sticks and stones may break my bones, but words will never hurt me." As much as she believed him then, now she knew it was a mindless and empty trope.

The bruise on her leg will heal and be forgotten; Pat's words were indelible. Yet, despite the crushing rebuke, she knew, before she left Pat's house, she had to be one hundred per cent certain.

"I'm gonna say his name, Pat, just nod if it's him. I can't afford any more mistakes."

The bitter cud Pat chewed on still fed her bile. Her reply was spat out. "No, it's fuckin fireman Sam, now piss off."

The rear bay doors were open. All three machines were in their respective bays. The two pumps dripped water after the night's road dirt had been sluiced off. The ALP was bone dry, so a quiet night for that crew.

There he was, by his car, talking to his counterpart on the Blue.

They appear to be deep in conversation, thought Linsey, so she tried to slip by unnoticed.

"Oh, don't say good morning then."

"Sorry, didn't want to disturb you."

"The only time you disturb me is when your knots come undone." He referenced a recent knots and lines drill they had.

Linsey looked at the two men smiling at her. This type of banter between all firefighters would constitute a normal day. Once acclimatised to it, it was water off a duck's back. It did, however, require a response.

"Yea well, practice makes perfect, eh?" With that, she turned on her heel and carried on into the station.

The two men watched her go.

"Looks like you touched a nerve there, Sean."

Sean watched her walk into the station. It angered him to see her fleece partially covering her firm arse while her blue jeans delineated her attractive legs to perfection. He turned to his counterpart.

"Women, eh? Can't live with them, can't kill 'em. Anyway, what was I saying?"

After the routine appliance checks, Arthur sat the watch down and went over the latest routine orders and his plan for the day ahead, providing the good citizens of Langden didn't require their services.

"And last but not least," said Arthur. "Sid Middlemarch is retiring."

"Sidney Middlemarch, we done our driving course together," said Ken.

"Was that horses?" Billy Butler quipped.

Ken ignored Billy before continuing.

"I thought he was dead. Where's he stationed?"

"Harlow," said Arthur, getting up from his chair. Ken puffed out some air.

"Harlow, can't go all that way for a do."

"Not even for a free bar?" Harryoo asked.

"And petrol; he'll pay for your travelling as well," added Perry. Eddie smiled. He liked it when the days started like this.

The empty mugs were placed on the aluminium tray and taken into the kitchen by Jim, the duty man. Ken started discussing the menu with Gretchen while the rest of the watch shuffled from the mess room to the watch room. Going out to the appliance bay on an autumnal morning to start work on the daily routines had to be done in stages.

Linsey was in the locker room. She pulled on her NATO jumper and, with a hand on her keys, hesitated before securing the locker door. She stared into the metallic dark green cabinet, her mind not functioning. There were her manuals, toiletries, a towel, and her small rucksack, all squashed in beside her clean fire gear. Stuck on the inside of her locker door were photos of the two most important men in her life. Her father and Robbie Williams. She would always love her father, but what of Robbie, always? Yea, they would grow old together. Her eyes scanned back to the rucksack.

Linsey ran her hand over the dark blue material. This soft, inanimate bag had no special place in her heart, contained no talismanic qualities other than memories. Picking it up from her bed before going away for a long weekend in Amsterdam with her housemates, or emptying out the Christmas presents she'd bought for her family. She looked at the bag and wanted to step into her memories; either one, it didn't matter, just to be anywhere other than here. This man had despoiled her workplace, her life. She knew it was him, just knew. She was tough, she reassured herself, could hold her own while knowing she wouldn't say anything.

Sean, however, held all the aces, was in a position of power, was established, was liked, and was a man. What would the rest of the watch think if she started making waves after five minutes? 'Typical, women, and a grass! Fucking women always a problem in any organisation'.

She quelled these thoughts. Her silence, though, brought her no comfort or justice for Pat; it did provide protection while the knowledge she held was, like her cherished possessions, secure inside.

Linsey closed the door on happier times and heard Flo, the cleaner, in the toilets. She went to say hello.

"Eat shit," said Flo pouring bleach down the pan. Flo had been told not to use the chemical but if the bosses thought she was spending her time scrubbing crap off porcelain, they had another thing coming.

"Morning, Flo."

"Oh, morning, darling. What do this lot live on? Fuck sake. Look at this." Flo knocked open the door to one of the toilet stalls and pointed.

Linsey didn't particularly want to look but felt compelled out of sisterhood. "Look at it, it's like an ancient fuckin club, it won't flush."

Linsey wanted to laugh, not at Flo's work predicament, just her accurate description.

Flo looked at Linsey and could see the laughter hiding behind her eyes. She was disappointed.

"It's alright for you, darling, you don't have to deal with this shit. It's the second one this week. I'm going to the ADO, he can fuckin deal with it." Linsey looked at Flo and thought again about women in the workplace. All in all, it was just shit.

Flo closed the door on her problem, then nudging Linsey with her elbow, said, "'Ere, it weren't you, was it?"

Perry stuck his head around the corner.

"What you two laughing at? Lins, Sean wants you."

Linsey's laughter turned cold.

"What's he want?"

"I dunno, best you cut along and find out, and if you don't mind, ladies, I need the loo."

Flo reopened the door.

"'Ere are, use this one."

The staircase formed the central core of the building. At its base, a firefighter could turn right or left to access the bay. Straight ahead across the carpeted foyer is the office of the ADO. The open door allowed Linsey a coup d'oeil of its occupants and the power therein. Behind his desk sat ADO Clarence Siddall. He appeared in general discussion with Eddie and Chris, and though the conversation was above her pay grade, she wanted to join them. To ask if she could sit in the corner, not say anything, not listen, just be in the presence of men she trusted.

"Ah, Linsey, are you ok? You look lost," said Arthur Church.

"Er, no, I'm alright. Thanks, Guv, blonde moment."

"Oi, none of that sexist talk, please; trying to eradicate that language in the workplace. Well, on this watch at least."

Good luck with that, thought Linsey. "I'm looking for Sean, he wants me for something."

"Well, it was I who thought you should join him; he is in my office. Two carers have brought in an old fella who needs a ring cut off. Have you seen or done such a thing yet?"

"No, Guv."

"Well, it's another service we provide, so please join him. It's time I ushered the rest of your colleagues out to their jobs in the bay. Should be fun, like herding sheep."

On another day, the candour bestowed on her by Arthur would mean another level of acceptance attained. Right now, she felt terribly alone. Laughter from the watch room made her feel excluded. No one really needed her, so why not walk out the door, get in her car, and go? It's a job, just a job, nothing else. Go back to driving for a living. She yearned for the boredom of the cab.

"Ah, Linsey, this is John, and he's got a very sore finger."

Linsey had stepped into the station officer's office. Sean had his hand on an elderly male in a wheelchair. He sat slumped, with his chin on his chest, a ball of a man with a rubber spine. Two women in pink overalls, black slacks, and trainers duetted a good morning.

"Am I right in saying this is your first time, Linsey?" Sean asked. He turned to the carers.

"Linsey is our newest recruit."

"Ooh, first time for everything, Cath."

Cath smiled at her colleague's innuendo but maintained her decorum.

Instead, she squatted in front of John and tried to get his attention. While caressing his cheek, she spoke to Sean and Linsey.

"He's been pulling at it for a while, and as you can see, sore and swollen." The nameless carer rolled her eyes at Sean but refrained from further comment.

"May I," said Linsey, taking Cath's place. She gently held John's hand in hers. The knuckle of his wedding finger was twice its normal size. If one were to oil paint an anatomical sketch of John's hand, maroon and blue would be required. The thick gold band looked partially buried in the contused flesh, though it hadn't broken the skin.

"Hello, John. That looks painful, but we are going to do our best to get that off your finger. Ok?"

"He can't speak, love," said Cath. "Hasn't in years."

Sean was peeved that Linsey took command of the situation. He wanted to give her instructions that showcased his knowledge and know-how. He looked at both the carers.

"She has a way with men, young and old."

Sean and the nameless carer enjoyed a silent collusion.

Linsey picked up the ring cutter from the box on the desk.

"If you wouldn't mind holding his arm, Cath. Has he had any painkillers?"

"Paracetamol."

Linsey started talking to John as if he were fully compos mentis.

"John, I'm just going to slide this hook part under your wedding ring, then I'll start to gently turn this wheel like this, just like a tin opener, John, and we will get the ring off your finger."

As she explained, she carried out the manoeuvre, thankful to Eddie for showing it to her in one of their quieter moments.

The serrated wheel cut into the ring. A dusting of gold sparkled on the bruised skin.

The thickness of the ring meant it would take time. Linsey kept a steady rhythm going. She felt hot under the gaze of Sean and the carers. John never looked at her, never flinched.

"Would you like me to take over, Linsey?" Sean asked.

She shook her head.

"Nearly there, John," said Cath.

"Nearly there, John," mimicked the nameless carer as she looked over Cath's shoulder. She thought it was time to expose the room to her professionalism.

The precious groove deepened along with Linsey's resolve. She was pleased that her first attempt at cutting a ring off would be successful without Sean interceding.

With the slightest of jolts, the incision was complete. Linsey removed the cutter and, taking the ring delicately in the tips of her fingers, prised open the malleable metal.

John breathed out a sigh and, on that audible breath, came the first word he had spoken in years.

"Fuck!"

"John, darling," said Cath, hugging him.

Linsey stood up as the nameless carer threw an arm around her shoulders, simultaneously looking at Sean.

"He spoke," she said. "Well done, amazing."

"Yea, amazing," said Sean in a voice devoid of emotion.

Linsey and Sean stood together in the yard and half waved, half nodded as the carers drove away with a relieved John.

"Care in the community."

"What?" Linsey replied.

"Not just fires and rescues," continued Sean, "but care in the fucking community. Still, that's what you're good at, eh, Linsey, caring for all the lost souls."

Sean had detected the change in Linsey's demeanour since the start of the shift. He knew why, knew she had been in contact with Pat. Therefore, a change of tactic was required. No more Mr nice guy. This bitch needed controlling and to be put in her place.

"I'm going in, help the others with the routines."

"You'll go when I tell you to go, firefighter. There are a couple of lengths of hose around the back of the tower, dropped off by Leigh. Come and help me with them."

All stations possessed their own complement of hose. Linsey knew that if the hose belonging to this station had been left at a fire for operational reasons, then it would be delivered by the last station to leave the incident. If that was in the middle of the night, then they would sling it around the back of the tower, save disturbing the sleeping watch.

As she walked to the far side of the yard, the tower loomed over her. She looked up, it started to fall; she would be crushed. Her level of anxiety was creating a visual vertigo. She looked down and focused on the ground. She could see the cold aluminium male coupling attached to the end of a coiled length of hose, the colour of blood protruding from the back of the tower. Her breathing was shallow, the cold air only reaching the top of her lungs. Each footstep felt the concrete through the soles of her work shoes. Linsey wanted to kneel and feel the concrete with her hands, lay her cheek on the floor, perhaps then someone would come to help.

Where were they? All her friends are just a few metres away in the bay. Ken in the kitchen with Gretchen; Flo upstairs in the locker room. Where were Eddie and Chris? Couldn't they see her walking to the back of the tower with this maniac?

"Now, listen to me, you need to keep your cute little snout out of other people's business and just stick to your fucking job." They stood between the tower and the perimeter wall. She had heard of men coming here to sort out their differences. A stupid euphemism for stupid men whose only answer was to fight. She would give her high teeth for one of them now. To knock this bastard out. The thought created an adrenaline spike. Linsey clenched her fists but retaliated with her tongue.

"I know about you, Sean, I know how you treated Pat's sister, what you done to her."

"You know fuck all about me, you little cunt."

His face was inches from hers. His breath smelled of stale tea. A fleck of spittle landed on her chin; she felt sick.

"If you so much as breath a word about this," he made to head butt her, stopping short.

"You will be out of this job; your feet won't touch the fucking ground." A car horn sounded.

"Oi, did you win your fucking licence in a lottery, pal?"

On the other side of the perimeter wall, a driving altercation was taking place. "Yea, dream on, wanker."

Sean was listening to the argument. Distracted from his own. Linsey wanted to laugh at this black comedy.

Sean re-focused,

"I know people, understand?"

Linsey nodded.

"Now, pick up that hose and put it in the hose store on the shelf for testing." With that, he was gone.

The hose store is at the far end of the appliance bay. Inside, the station's hose complement sits on sturdy wooden shelving like coils of red liquorice. These were in addition to the hose on the machines. Each length of hose was numbered, and a corresponding tally was placed on a board affixed to the wall. This board showed the whereabouts of all the hoses, for instance, whether it be on a lorry, in store or away for repair.

Linsey had placed the seventy-millimetre hose on the appropriate shelf and was looking for its corresponding tally. Her back was to the door.

"Oi Oi, Lazy, so this is where you're hiding."

Linsey never looked around. She flicked a forefinger over each cheek and sniffed.

"Alright, Puke, you know, just carrying out orders."

Luke picked up on the flat tone in her voice. He came and stood next to her.

"What one you looking for?"

"12493"

"How's tricks?"

"Yea, sweet, thanks."

Luke tended to use words like a blunt instrument, but he was married with children, and he had learnt to detect the differences in the female psyche and empathise accordingly.

"You on blob?"

"I've never envied Alice, Puke, but I have to admit, she is one lucky girl."

"Try my best."

Luke picked up the tally and moved it to the correct column.

"And women say we can't find anything. Can I get you a cup of tea?"

The offer of a simple act of kindness flooded her emotions. The dam never broke, but the waters crested and fell. Linsey cuffed at her cheeks with her sleeve.

When Chris walked into the hose store, he was confronted with Luke, arms wrapped around Linsey.

Luke pointed downwards and mouthed as if speaking through glass.

"She's got the painters in."

"Hi, Ed, it's Jane."

Eddie was sitting in his room, catching up on paperwork that no one would ever look at, when his phone rang.

"Hello, Jane. How are you? How is Nev? How's he doing?"

It was difficult for him to hide the delight this call brought him. Jane could tell. She loved Eddie's child-like equality when it bubbled to the surface. It reminded her of the childhood they could never leave.

"I'm fine and Nev is doing much better, not out of the woods yet but better."

"That's great, Jane, great. I have been, you know…" He faltered.

"What?"

"I have been thinking of you, both."

"Well, we have been thinking about you, Ed, and talking about you."

"Oh."

He didn't know if he could take another tongue-lashing.

"Yea, we both feel we didn't treat you very well when you came here last and wondered if you would come to lunch this Saturday?"

"Yea, love to yea; that's great, that's…"

He stopped waffling. Did he hear that familiar chuckle?

"What?"

"Nothing, see you at twelve."

"Is it him?" Chris asked.

Linsey shook her head, pinching her nose between thumb and forefinger, then wiping her hand on her overall trousers. This world was of her own making, and she would deal with it on her own.

They looked out of the store room window across the hard, cold yard toward the tower and the scene of the crime.

How many crimes had he committed, and how many more does he get to commit, she wondered. Luke had gone to make some tea.

"I can do things, Linsey, get the ball rolling, but you have to speak first, to me and Eddie."

"No."

"This is silly. Listen, remember the other night at the caravan fire, you were willing to call him out for me, now I'm saying the same to you. What's changed?"

"Plenty."

She looked at the windowsill in front of her. A bee exhausted from head-butting the glass pane had lain down and died without looking for another way out. She looked at Chris for the first time.

"What did you say to me at that fire, Chris, eh? I can fight my own corner, that's what you said. Well, so can I, Chris."

"Ok, but he's a nasty piece of work."

"Tell me about it."

"Look, I shouldn't tell you this, but I've been asking around."

"And?"

"We never really knew how we got him. Why he's here or if he actually wanted this watch, and he's as fucking vague as an embarrassing symptom."

Chris looked back at the door.

"Turns out, on his last watch, he was seeing the sister of one of the firefighters. All was well until one day he knocked her about. The firefighter had to be pulled off him in the watch room."

"And that's it?"

"Generally, yea, that's it. Sweep it under the carpet, move the problem on, or in this case, both of them on."

"So, they moved the firefighter too, fuck sake."

Knowledge is power; however, this made her feel weaker still.

"What about Arthur? He must know."

"Arthur is a very astute guvner, Lins. He doesn't say much, but he watches and listens, always knows when there is something in the air. Eddie and I had asked him about Sean, and he refused to comment. I think he is keen to be seen as impartial for now, just in case, but don't think for one minute he would be disinterested if the true Sean Stolly reared his ugly head on this watch. Perhaps, that's why we should act."

Linsey shook her head. "You won't, and I've told you I'm not."

Luke walked in with two steaming mugs of tea.

"There ya go, Lins."

"Thanks."

Chris watched the transaction.

"So, just the two mugs then."

"Fuck me," said Luke handing over his tea to Chris before turning back to the kitchen. "Your time of the month also."

39

Ray looked at his wrist, now that the plaster had been removed. The pallid skin was dry and had an odour unfamiliar to him. It looked thinner, and the bony ache informed him of the coming winter. He rubbed the repair with a satisfaction long overdue.

He should phone Eddie and tell him, but he knew if he missed the call, he'd panic, thinking something was wrong. No, he would wait to mention it next time his son called him.

Ray had started to feel more settled in his new home. His early misgivings, like the morning frost, had evaporated. He had convinced himself that his broken wrist was celestial punishment for selling the family home in Stanford le Hope.

"The body is wonderful at repair, normally making the bone stronger than before."

The doctor's words were a boon. His fractured past, once broken, was now restored. He must make contact with old acquaintances at the Con club, take Eddie along. That would be amusing. His son would rail against the very idea, then acquiesce to please him in their newfound relationship. Maybe he would bring Charlotte. Ray hadn't met her yet, but from what he had been told by his son, the expectation would be worth the wait. To see his son with a partner would be unique. His son had always kept that part of his life closely guarded, and why not? Both of his parents had done the same. He with his weekends in London and his mother with her weekends to god knows where.

Eddie had learnt from the best. Jane was the only one he had known. Poor deluded Jane, who as a kid thought she had the measure of the Hart household. When, as an adult, all was revealed to her, an unbridgeable chasm had opened between her and Eddie.

In the kitchen, Ray filled the kettle with enough water for one cup, the weight of which hurt his arm. He looked out the kitchen window, admiring a ferocious Robin as it defended its territory from a would-be usurper. The sweet-looking bird would fight to the death for what it considered to be its. *Looks can be deceiving*, thought Ray.

The steam bubbles crackled as the water boiled. He poured the water into the cup and said, "Four minutes," out loud.

Where was he? Ah, Eddie and Jane. He knew she had always held a candle for Eddie, but what of his son? Had he ever glanced back over his shoulder and wondered what might have happened if he had chosen a different path, not the one least trodden, the lonelier one? Is that what he had bequeathed his son, loneliness? Had he raised a boy devoid of feeling?

He may have, but Eve more than made up for it; she overflowed with passion, especially for her boy. Perhaps, then, it's in his DNA and from the moment of conception, his direction in life had been mapped. Either way, it saddened him. Ray lifted the tea bag and squeezed it between his thumb and forefinger. Meeting Charlotte might give him a clue.

40

It was cold but mild for the time of year; chilly, a nip in the air, a bit parky. The residents of Langden proffered their opinions of the weather to one another as they prepared for Christmas. Enthusiasts were covering their houses with countless bulbs and filling the front garden with dubious associations to the birth of Christ. Carols and festive pop songs rang out from shops keen to help customers part with their hard-earned cash. Parcels were sent, deliveries made. Things were wrapped and hidden. The town was busy. That included the industrial parks where companies, large and small, raced to complete their work before the holidays started in earnest.

Silva's was one such firm. Situated on the Northfleet site, it occupied the last unit to be built there. It was furthest from the main road and was fenced off along two sides from scrub land that led down to Shell Haven Creek. It was also the largest unit, brick built to door height, then metal clad. A number 16 hung next to the larger sectional, up and over door and in the corner, the front entrance for visitors was adjacent to a small ground-floor office. Silva's printed supplements and flyers for the local free papers. The presses ran through the night and by four in the morning, the product was in the delivery vans.

This just left Albie to secure the premises and remain on site until mid-morning or the threat of intruders had passed. Previous break-ins had all taken place in the early hours between the finished print run and the neighbouring units opening up.

Albie, a man of a certain age, lived with his spinster sister in the oldest bungalow in Old Street. It's where they were born and raised, and upon the death of their parents, both could see no reason to leave.

The younger Albie dug holes for the GPO. His forearms resembled Popeye's, and his back described a question mark. He had never sought a soulmate, having found the perfect partner in alcohol. When his sister saw the solace it brought her brother, she followed suit, and their controlled sipping maintained a functioning life with all edges rounded.

Albie could retire, but the lack of routine scared him; he knew the bottle would then demand more of his time, so he would drive to work every night until the day he lost his licence and his job.

Once there, his night consisted of sweeping up, making tea, and goffering for the men. By five in the morning, he was alone in the building. He would check that the unit was secure before settling down in the small office on the raised storage area at the rear of the shop floor. His routine never changed, which was a shame because if it had, if he had thought to do one more sweep of the site, he might have noticed that one of the guys had left a small heater on at a work station. An area kept meticulously clean and tidy except for a large cleaning cloth that had fallen to the floor in front of the heater and had already, as Albie poured a healthy tot of whiskey into his black coffee, begun to reach the critical surface temperature whereupon it would ignite.

The fire service, steeped in history, has its share of archaic terms. The bells going down being one such example. Throughout history, the bell has proved an effective method of raising the alarm, and though no longer used in the modern stations of Essex, the term has proved to be more resilient. Now, an electronic wail accompanied by emergency lighting gave fair warning to the Red Watch. At the time of actuation, the firefighters were dispersed around the station. Arthur was talking to ADO Clarence Siddall, Eddie was on the phone to Charlotte, while Chris and Lindsey were still in the hose store.

Jim was looking at the riders' board for the following day, and Harry and Adam chatted idly in the watch room. Ken was making sandwiches and baguettes while grazing on cheese and ham. Perry and Billy were under the bonnet of Luke's car. Luke was behind the wheel, gunning the engine. That left Sean. He was in the leading firefighter's room, the one he shared with Chris. He sat at the desk, looking out the window and across to the far end of the bay where he knew Chris and Lindsey were ensconced. His forefinger picked at dry skin on the edge of his thumbnail.

Fucking bitches, bane of my life, he thought, *demanding, high maintenance and divisive.* Work used to be a sanctuary, respite from all their whingeing, whining, fucking moaning ways. Not anymore. Now they invade one of the last bastions of male life, turning up with their sense of entitlement and pathetic mewling tropes.

'We just want to be treated the same, have the same opportunities, same rights'.

Like fuck they do, they want to take over. They should know their place. What was it dad used to say? 'A good woman should be a cook in the kitchen and a whore in bed, nothing a slap won't cure'.

Dad had it right, and mum too; she served her man. He, Sean, served the public, a life of service, and behind every man should be a good woman serving him. They needed teaching and men who were not prepared to teach them were weak, like that fucking pansy Chris.

Sean's thoughts were fuelling his anger. He knew he had to be careful. If it got him in trouble again, his father's Masonic influence could be exhausted, and his reputation would soil the family name. Reputations precede you in this job. Word gets around. He had to be careful.

But that bitch, that fucking bitch…

His thought was interrupted as the bells went down and called him once again to serve the public. All of them.

Arthur dismounted from the cab, stood in front of the building on fire, and looked. From the rear of the unit on the right-hand side, a thick black cloud of smoke had broken through a skylight and was rising fast. The solid column of toxic filth rose high into a cloudless sky. The light breeze was taking it across the marshes to the river.

He was joined by his officers.

"At least it's not going towards the town, Guv. How many do you want to make it?" Chris said.

Arthur considered how many pumps he might need initially.

"Let's start with five, Chris."

Chris left to send the priority message to control.

"We got plenty of water, Arthur, big hydrant on the corner. Luke and Billy are setting in. It's going well, eh?" Eddie said.

"Excuse me, gents, I've got the place next door, should I be worried?"

"Not unless this lot goes bang, and can you stop those forklifts? I don't want them running over the hose," said Arthur.

"Yea, of course."

Arthur continued.

"Does he have anything that could go bang, acetylene for instance?"

"Nah, Frank don't use any of that, he's in the print."

"Where is he?"

"I phoned him straight after I put the call in, he's still an hour away." People have their priorities and they differ according to one's needs, demands, and expectations.

The man who owned the unit next to the conflagration had his. His livelihood and that of his employees were foremost on his list. He was not, however, uncaring and wanted to assist as best he could.

"Just one more thing, one of my forklift drivers said that car there belongs to Frank's night watchman, and he's normally gone by now." Arthur looked at the man with a studied incredulity.

Chris arrived back.

"I've sent the priority, Guv."

"Thanks, Chris; send another, 'Persons Reported'."

"Ok."

"Eddie, get your BA crew ready to go in. I reckon the office door is our best bet."

Arthur turned back to the businessman who had been listening intently to this esoteric world that few people are ever privy to.

"So, you reckon the key holder is an hour away?"

"Yea, forty-five minutes maybe."

"Do you know the layout in there?" Arthur asked.

"Not a clue, but one of my blokes used to work for Frank, I'll get him."

The noise level, as on any fire ground, started to increase. The building on fire cried out in pain. The ALP's diesel engine roared as it raised the platform up over the scene, the water tender's pump was revving high, keen to compete. Firefighters were shouting commands and asking questions. Areas of command and control were being set up, and in the distance, the two-tone sound of the additional fire appliances ordered by Arthur was adding to the urgent cacophony. The 'Persons Reported' message would bring the police and ambulance.

Meanwhile, Eddie was walking over to Perry and Linsey, his BA crew. This was a time he had always secretly wanted to swerve. He was going to put Linsey into a dangerous situation. He could never justify swapping her for one of the blokes; that decision would be met with derision and disdain. He had to tell himself it wasn't warranted, but couldn't stop the feeling in the pit of his stomach rebelling against his irrational thought.

Perry and Linsey stood by the lorry with their BA sets on their backs, waiting to see if they were going to be needed inside the building or whether Eddie would tell them to get their sets off, they were just going to bollock the water on from the outside.

As he approached, they could tell from his demeanour that it wasn't good. "Its persons reported, the night watchman might be in there." They were joined by Sean.

"You putting them in, Ed?"

"Yea."

A muffled explosion came from inside the building. They turned in unison to see the smoke column mushrooming into a soft pillow of orange and black before it assumed its original solid bar.

Sean looked at Linsey with cold satisfaction. "I'll run the BA board, Eddie," he said.

"No, you get rigged as well. I want a team of three in there for this one. I'll get a leading hand from one of the oncoming crews to run the BA board." Perry knew this made sense and felt more at ease with the decision to go in. He started pulling on his snood and closing his tunic fully to give himself maximum protection against the heat that he knew awaited him.

Linsey felt sick at the thought of being in a dangerous situation with Sean, a man who despised her. Once as a teenager, she sat in the back of a car that was speeding too fast with a moron trying to run his hand between her legs. Telling the driver she was about to throw up in his daddy's car allowed her and her friend to escape to a nearby chip shop and the comfort of strangers until the morons drove off.

As the bile rose in her throat, she knew any lame excuse would end her career. She glanced at Perry, busying himself with his personal protection and wondered how he felt inside.

Despite all their training and safety procedures endlessly drummed into them, despite the cover they gave to one another, that very ethos of 'you go I go' despite the years of experience, the essence of which can never be taught, contained in the collective mind of the officers in charge, she knew danger awaited.

That was ok, all of that would be ok if Sean had been removed from the ominous equation. The kernel of doubt she had in his trust was undermining everything else. Could he be that evil? She forced herself to concentrate on the things she could control—pulling the snood over her head, closing her tunic tight around her neck, tightening the straps of her breathing apparatus, turning her torch on that hung on the right side of her chest, touching the personal line in its pouch that could be connected to a partner so they would never be separated in the blind world they operated in.

Billy and Luke were sweating cobs. They had run sixty metres back to the hydrant carrying the hydrant key and bar and lengths of seventy mil hose. Billy levered the hydrant cover plate out of the ground, dropped to his knees, and reached into the small pit to remove the blank cap covering the hydrant outlet. Luke then connected the standpipe, cracking it open and letting a brown sludge of water momentarily spill out until it ran clear. They both ran out a length of hose from the double-headed standpipe before returning to their lorry for two more lengths, which they connected to the first two.

They repeated this once more before two lines of red hose snaked their way from the hydrant to the back of the pump. Luke then ran again and turned the water on, giving Harry, the pump operator, an unlimited supply for the BA crew and the Alp, which they also connected with a hose. From a side locker on the pump, they ran out a hose reel to the front door of the premises, where Jim and Adam were trying to crowbar it open.

For a brief moment, Billy and Luke stood watching Jim and Adam, both were blowing, hard.

Eddie came up to the four firefighters.

"Luke, go and get a sledgehammer."

"Ok." Luke ran off.

"Billy, go and tell that crew that just arrived, I want an officer to run BA control and an emergency BA crew standing by."

"Ok." Billy ran off.

Eddie turned at the sound of wood splintering as the door opened. Jim and Adam stood back as black smoke billowed out.

Luke arrived with the large hammer. "Don't need it?" He asked needlessly.

"No, thanks, Luke, put it back before we lose it," replied Eddie.

Luke took a breath before returning the heavy piece of equipment to its rightful place.

High above it all, Chris, in conjunction with Ken far below, was busy manoeuvring the ariel platform as close as possible to the hole in the roof where the products of combustion were rising angrily into the friendly skies. He was tasked with aiming a jet of water onto the fire as best he could. The light breeze was bending the smoke column away from him, but he knew full well that Mother Nature could turn on him in an instant and envelop him in hot poison. It would then be Ken's responsibility to get the platform into the fresh air immediately. For now, he wanted to plop a jet of water into the burning building while keeping himself at a safe distance. The explosion a minute ago warned him not to go too close.

The three-person BA team stood near their entry point. They listened to Arthur's instructions.

"Right, I've had it on reasonably good authority that if he's in there, then he is more than likely in a small office, come the tea room at the rear of the unit. It's on a raised storage area. The good news," Arthur said it without a trace of irony, "is, it is located on this left-hand side, whereas the seat of the fire appears. I reiterate appears to be on the right side. I want you to go in and carry out a left-hand search, working your way down to the office. There should be a fire exit in that area, but the side of this unit is so overgrown, it's difficult to tell for sure. I'll have a team start to clear the bushes and hopefully get to it for you."

"Maintain radio contact, I want to know if you find him or not. Sean, you lead, then Linsey, then Perry. Linsey, assist Sean with the search and help Perry pulling the hose reel along. If you see the fire and can give it a drink, do so, but your main task is to locate this bloke. Understood?" All three nodded.

Arthur looked around to make sure everything was in position, acknowledged Eddie, then walked off to speak with ADO Clarence Siddall, who had just arrived and could be seen standing by the open boot of his car, hastily dressing in his fire gear.

Eddie took over where Arthur had left off.

"Stick together and check your gauges constantly. The first one of you to reach the turn-round point on your gauge, tell the other two, then get yourselves out, fuck the rescue."

As harsh as his comment sounded, his crew came first. It also gave the team permission to put their safety first and not risk doing something foolhardy. They had now been at the incident for nine minutes.

The fire was well established. For now, it was in charge, it had everything it needed, as fuel and oxygen were in abundance. Palettes of paper were licked then consumed; metal shelving twisted, throwing chemicals into the mix; plastic machine guards caught then dripped goblets of flame. Surfaces fumed before bursting into action, and all the time, it got hotter. The top half of the building was comprised of metal cladding. The area directly involved started to glow. This intense heat radiated along the walls and roof, turning unit sixteen into an oven.

Sean, Linsey, and Perry entered this inferno. If Albie was shut inside that office, then there was a chance he had enough protection and oxygen to still be alive. They had to try.

At first, the heat didn't seem too bad. They were completely covered by their fire gear. The heat would take hold of them gradually. Sean immediately located the external wall to his left and kept in constant contact with it as they made their way into the building. He carried the hose reel branch. Linsey stayed close to him; her personal line was attached to his BA harness. She pulled on the hose reel, helping Perry drag it with them as they inched along. At first, it wasn't so bad. Jim and Adam were by the entrance, feeding the hose reel in as best they could, but the further they went, the more difficult it became. The line of hose resisted every change of direction and caught on the machinery.

Linsey found it impossible to stay close to Sean and turn and help Perry pull the hose through. She uncoupled her personal line from Sean but couldn't feed it back in the small pouch with her gloved hands. Sean was shouting at her. She couldn't make out what he was saying. He sounded underwater. All she could hear enclosed in her face mask was her own breathing as it became more laboured. She dropped her personal line and let it trail on the floor. Now, it was getting hot. If they had been pulling a hose reel around corners and general obstructions outside on a cool day, they would sweat. Now, completely covered in thick protective clothing, wearing breathing apparatus inside a building on fire, their tee shirts and overall trousers were soaked through.

A firefighter's sweat had been known to get so hot that it blistered the skin. Perry worked relentlessly. He seemed to disappear, then the hose would bunch up around Linsey before Sean inched forward again. Visibility was poor. Off to their right, there was an orange inky glow, in front a swallowing blackness.

"Gauges!"

It was the first word Perry had shouted. Linsey grabbed Sean and shone her torch on her gauge.

The three stood close together, each read their gauge and shouted the result.

"We've got to get that sectional door open," said Eddie to Arthur and Clarence, "or we are never gonna get serious water on the fire."

"We should put a team in on a right-hand search, they'll get to the inside of that door within ten metres, try to open it." Eddie looked at the two senior officers.

"Do it," said Clarence.

"Have we heard from Sean?" Arthur asked Eddie.

"Yea, not very clear but we can hear him."

"Fucking portable radios, shit," replied Arthur.

"They ain't that fucking good," said Eddie.

Having read their gauges and deciding they could continue, Sean turned and walked straight into a mess of wiring that had fallen across their path. With one hand, he tried to free himself. The wires from the dead emergency lighting circuit had come adrift. It caught on his BA harness, snaring him with dangerous ease. He dropped the hose reel and, with both hands, started pulling at the wires. He stepped backwards, knocking into Linsey. He felt the wires snag the raised visor on his helmet. He turned around in a vain attempt to free himself, which exacerbated the situation.

Rational thought can be the first casualty when working hard in extreme heat.

"Fuck sake, argh."

Sean had stopped thinking. His swinging arm caught Linsey across the chest, knocking her back. The heel of her boot hit the hose reel and she started to fall. Her BA cylinder hit something solid, twisting her sideways. She fell to the ground, jarring her elbow and hip. Before the pain registered, Perry was pulling her to her feet. Next, he grabbed Sean, pinning his arms.

"Sean!" He yelled. "Stop! I'm gonna cut the wires. Lins, shine your torch here. Good."

The thin cables gave way to Perry's blade as he picked and pulled them apart, slowly releasing Sean from the web that held him.

"Gauges," shouted Perry. They checked their gauges to see how much air they had left. Perry was close to his turn-round point.

"Let's get out of here," shouted Sean.

Perry looked at Sean, and there, just over his shoulder, he saw the stairs. "Look, the stairs; let's try and get him," said Perry. "Come on."

All three heaved the hose reel to the bottom of the stairs. Halfway up, the stairs disappeared in hot, dense smoke. The heat in this corner of the building was intense. Linsey had never felt so hot, so enclosed. She wanted to rip her mask off in a desperate hope of something cool. Then, a sudden explosion of light hit her eyes. Sean had located the emergency exit door and had knocked it open. Their eyes adjusted to green, unkempt bushes and blue sky. In a few steps, they could be standing outside in fresh, cool air, their masks off, wiping sweat from their eyes.

"Come on, let's get up there and see if we can get him," shouted Perry. He led the way up the stairs.

For Linsey, going up the stairs and not out the exit was one of the hardest things she had ever done. She looked at Sean. He said nothing, just stared back. She started to ascend back into the darkness, tapping Perry's heel to let him know she was there.

The inside of the small office was smoke-filled and coal black; the heat was brutal. Life in this room had long ceased to be tenable. Together, they felt their way around, defining an object by its shape and weight. Linsey ran her hand over a ribbed surface, realising it was a draining board, before knocking a kettle into the sink.

"Linsey," Perry was shouting. She reached out and down, locating Perry as he was pulling the lifeless body of Albie from under the table. He had him under the arms. Linsey made to grab the legs when a massive explosion ripped through the office. Linsey fell to the floor as the ceiling fell in, covering them in debris. When she opened her eyes, it was lighter. Part of the main roof had collapsed, releasing huge volumes of smoke. She got to her knees, no extra pain. She could move, she could breathe, good. It was then she saw the large metal girder lying across the room and across Albie and Perry. She stepped over the girder and knelt by Perry's head.

"Perry, Perry."

"I'm ok, I think."

"I'll get Sean."

The flimsy office was destroyed, but the metal platform and stairs were still intact. She descended them as quickly as possible. She could see the open emergency exit, the green and blue beyond. She looked about her, but what she couldn't see was Sean. She called his name, realising how stupid it was. So much smoke had escaped with the collapse that a lot of the area was now visible. She saw the hose reel on the floor. Picking it up, she heaved it back up the stairs with her. At the top of the stairs, she adjusted the branch of the hose reel to spray, then opened it up. The powerful spray would clear more smoke from the immediate area. She then tried to lift the girder, but it was beyond her. She went and sat next to Perry.

"Are you in pain?"

"No, I think I'm alright, he has taken the full force of it."

Linsey looked at the dead man lying face down over Perry's body. The steel beam across his back. She was glad she couldn't see his face.

"Where's Sean?"

"Gone for help."

"Gauges," said Perry.

She checked hers, then his. Perry's was low but lying still would reduce his consumption. Sean would explain everything, and help would be here in no time, so she would just sit here with her partner and wait. Everything will be fine. She looked down at Perry lying so still, eyes open, staring at nothing. She thought of his wife and what she might be doing right now. Linsey reached and took hold of Perry's hand.

You go I go, she thought.

41

Once the large sectional door was opened, the fire could be hit easily with a couple of seventy-millimetre hose lines. It died quickly under the deluge. Chris came down from his eyrie, and before he could ask about the BA crew, the ALP was ordered to a flat fire in a high-rise in Chelmsford. It took the best part of an hour to get the fire under control. As the ALP drove away from the incident, it passed a private ambulance from the local undertakers arriving for the deceased. Some of the fire crews took their first opportunity for a break, passing around the bottled water they carried. They stood bunched up in their yellow helmets; hence, the nickname bestowed on them by the other emergency services, Daffodils.

Arthur and Eddie were discussing how many pumps would be needed for the relief. This was the number of fire appliances required to take over from the five currently in attendance.

"Two should do it," said Eddie.

"Yea, two should do it."

Eddie looked at Arthur.

"What do you think of Sean's action?" He tried to sound non-committal.

"I know what you're thinking, Eddie, but let's face it, he made a snap decision to leave them and get help, and we did get to them quickly because of that."

"Don't you think together Linsey and he could have shifted that beam?" Arthur shrugged.

"Decisions, decisions, eh, there for the grace of god go I." Eddie turned, but before he could go to send the message for the relief crews, Arthur grabbed hold of his shoulder.

"It's never easy, is it, Eddie? Sending a crew in."

Both men stood in front of the burnt-out wreck of a building, now issuing a more friendly miasma.

"The people we spend so much time with, people we call friends, then we look them cold in their eyes before committing them to a hell. I've never found it easy, Eddie, and, after today, I know it will be harder. This job can take a lot from a person, but it does it slowly; a little bite here, a nibble there, until one day, you realise there's a part of you missing."

"Perhaps, we should stop sooner."

"How can we, Eddie? Tell me how."

Eddie looked at his guvner and searched for an answer that didn't come.

"I'll send that message, Arthur."

Arthur pursed his lips and nodded.

"Shall I inform Clarence first?"

"No need, Eddie, he's on the way to the hospital."

42

Perry and Linsey were sitting side by side on a bed. They had bypassed triage and were in the assessment unit waiting to be seen by a doctor.

"So, you went back down the stairs and told Sean what had happened, and he went for help?"

"Yea, that's it."

"Why didn't both of you come up and lift the girder off me?"

"I don't know. I can't remember properly for fuck sake, it's all a blur."

"Alright, keep your hair on."

Perry looked at Linsey. He thought about hugging her. Would he do that if it were Ken or Harry sitting next to him? Would he? Fuck.

"You look like shit," he said.

"You stink," she said.

"Hi, guys." Clarence Siddall pulled back the curtain.

"How are you both?"

"I'll be better when I can see a doctor and get out of here."

"Well, Perry, let's see what the doctor says, eh. They might want to keep you overnight."

"There is no way I'm staying here, Guv. Rachel hates me doing this job. If she found out I'd been hospitalised, she wouldn't rest until I quit. No way." Clarence knew further discussion was pointless.

"That's a nasty bruise on your arm, Linsey."

Linsey looked at the injury sustained in her fall.

"Yea, Guv, got it playing badminton."

"Badminton! Remind me never to partner with you."

Then took place the pregnant pause ubiquitous in every hospital visit while people search for something to say.

"Can I get you anything?" Clarence asked.

"Yea, a doctor, then a lift back to the station," replied a terse Perry.

It didn't take long for a doctor to give the all clear to Perry and Linsey, so once again, the Red Watch Langden were at full strength. The BA sets were cleaned and serviced, all equipment was checked, the lorries derved up and with the ALP back from Chelmsford, everything was ready to go again. Showers were hastily taken unless your name was Harry, who enjoyed a bit of a soak. Then, after he had slipped into his clean underwear, perfectly ironed tee, and overall trousers, he spent a while on his hair, finishing off with a dab of fou fou on each cheek. Tea was made, and dinner was being removed from the warming cabinet.

Linsey noticed Chris going into the leading firefighter's room. She followed. She wanted to tell him how good she felt and not to worry about her anymore. The incident had proven to her that she had the inner strength to do the job, but more than that, it had revealed to her—though she wouldn't tell Chris this part—that Sean, like all bullies, was a coward. At the crucial moment when his partners needed him, he ran. Sean knew she knew. She now had power over him. From the moment he left Perry and her in that building, he had freed her from any fear of him.

"Chris, my main man, that was a good job, eh?"

"Linsey, how can you say that? We could have lost you and Perry in that one."

"Nah, Perry got himself a bit squashed, but apart from that, we were fine." Her exuberant mood was making her lightheaded. She wanted to giggle with excitement. Getting Perry out safely, staying with him, the heat, the danger, the whole incident had created a euphoria within her. Tonight, she was getting pissed.

"Nah, sorry, Linsey. I don't see it like that."

"Why, Chris?"

"Because I saw everything. I was eighty feet up, remember. I saw him outside the building on his own with his mask off before the roof collapsed. He had left you two. Why, I don't know, but the roof collapse gave him the excuse he needed to run, run for help. That, on top of everything else recently, is enough. I'm going to Arthur with a formal complaint against him."

"Chris, he can't hurt us anymore. Things will be different, trust me."

"Hallo, what you two talking about?"

They turned to see that Sean had joined them.

"And what you doing in here? This is an officer's room."

"I invited her in. I wanted to talk to her about something."

"Oh yea, what?"

"Something, nothing to do with you."

"Well, maybe it is something to do with me. You two are always squirrelled away, making plans on your next move."

"You're talking out your arse, pal. I wouldn't waste my time doing anything that concerned you."

"Bollocks. I know you and your fag hag are up to something."

Chris hit him full in the face. Blood gushed from his broken nose as his head hit the floor with a dull thud.

Chris was about to follow it up with more, but Linsey stepped in front of him and shouted at him to stop. The commotion brought the passing ADO into the room.

"What the hell is going on?"

Chris was standing over Sean like Muhammad Ali stood over the prone Sonny Liston, except Muhammad never had Linsey Rivers pushing him away. Next to attend was Perry. He stuck his head inside the door, took one look at Sean, then said, "Looks like you're back up the hospital, Guv."

43

Eddie pulled up outside the house. He wasn't empty-handed for this visit, bringing with him a bunch of flowers and a Country Ramblers magazine. "Look what Eddie has brought you, darling, flowers," said Jane.

Eddie was still in the hallway, taking off his shoes. He walked into the lounge.

"It must be a laugh a minute living with her, Nev."

Nev was sitting in a high-backed chair that helped raise him to his feet when the button was pushed.

"Split me sides."

Nev's words were laboured but coherent. His health since their last meeting had markedly improved.

"Thanks."

Nev raised the magazine with his good hand.

"It's meant to inspire you to a full recovery, not rub salt in the wounds."

Eddie hoped the lopsided smile meant Nev concurred.

"Hope you're hungry. I've made a massive toad."

Jane was lifting the sausages in batter out of the oven as she spoke.

"Hank," replied Eddie.

The meal was a slow affair. Nev took his time over each small morsel, fastidiously wiping his mouth after each bite.

It pleased Eddie that Nev and Jane had let him into their inner sanctum. Let him witness the intimacy of carer and the cared for. *In sickness and in health*, he thought.

"That was delicious, thank you."

"You're welcome, Ed."

Jane was the only person who ever abbreviated his name to a single syllable. He liked it. It was another intimacy. One shared between the two of them. A shaft of wintry sunlight hit the table through the patio doors.

Secrets need light, thought Eddie.

"Nev, Jane is the only person to call me Ed, all the people I know, and they all call me Eddie, only Jane…"

"Charlotte," said Nev.

"Pardon."

"Uncle Ed."

"Oh yea, you're right." He was thrown. Not so much by the revelation, more by the name. Charlotte, his Charlotte. She called him Ed. He had forgotten. Forgotten about her today in his excitement at coming here to lunch. Moreover, he had not told her what he was doing. *Another secret hiding from the light*, he thought. Jane noticed the slight disconnect in Ed's demeanour and took over.

"How is your Charlotte?"

"Fine, thanks, good."

"You'll have to bring her over, introduce us. We'd like that, wouldn't we, Nev?" Nev nodded.

You lying cow, he thought. That was said for Nev's sake.

"Can we be honest?"

Eddie and Jane looked at Nev.

"Can I be honest? I have a problem with you, Eddie Hart. What's new, eh?" He wiped his mouth with a linen handkerchief.

"You know that, but still you came when we called, when we needed help; you were the only person who came without queshion or hesitation." Eddie tried to interject, but Nev raised a finger to his lips, demanding silence. "I'm not a fool. I know you came to help her." He glanced at his wife, who was looking down at the table.

"I know you would spend your days wiping my arse if she asked."

"Nev, please."

He reached out for her hand and gave it a squeeze.

"We asked you here today because I wanted to say thank you for helping my wife and to say you are welcome here, anytime. There."

Nev slumped back in the chair like a marionette rested by its controller.

The invisible arm string tightened, and he raised a hand to his forehead and gently wiped a forefinger over his eyebrow.

Jane got up and cupped her husband's face in her hands, kissing him on his cheek.

Eddie watched them both. He was humbled by a brave, gallant man, and he knew he was right. If Jane shouted jump, he'd ask how high. He was a slave, chained to his feelings, and he had never, as yet, been unfettered by another. He had tried, earlier this year, to walk away from them—at one point, thought he had succeeded with beautiful Charlotte—but like a moon caught in orbit, it was only time before he washed up here again. Was it love or the desire of unrequited love that hooked him? Was he destined to be unfulfilled as his parents were? Was that his legacy, a beneficiary of his parents' loveless marriage?

He looked at the empty plates and the uneaten food on Nev's. This is what Nev was offering, the crumbs from his table. Eddie looked at Jane. He had hurt her when he upped and left, taking his father to the city, then meeting Charlotte. Could he live off Nev's scraps if it helped Jane? If it helped them both?

"Cheesecake?"

"Why not?" Eddie said.

44

The smell of boiling cabbage assaulted Eddie as he stood in the hall, taking off his coat. He quickly opened Ray's bedroom door and placed his father's birthday present at the foot of his bed. In the kitchen, Ray was busy with their dinner. Pots steamed on the hob and condensation poured down the window.

"Hallo, Son, what are you doing?"

"Opening a window, it's like a sauna in here." "If you can't stand the heat, get out of my kitchen." Ray was in an ebullient mood.

"Apart from cabbage, which all the neighbours know we are having, what we got?"

"Toad in the hole, be ready in ten."

"Great! Had it yesterday."

"Well, you've got it again, won't kill ya."

"No, but the cabbage might turn it down before it turns to soup."

"Here." Ray handed his son a lager from the fridge.

"What on earth is this?"

"Polish, six per cent and cheap as chips. Now go and sit down, you're getting under my feet."

Eddie sat with his beer and, while he waited for dinner, surveyed the room. It was, as ever, very tidy. A place for everything and everything in its place. Still, it was different from his first visit. The sterile perfection of a show home was gone. A small pile of neatly folded newspapers were stacked on a chair, a large peace lily occupied a corner, and a colourful pashmina, no doubt his neighbour's, covered one arm of the sofa, quietly absorbing the odour of cabbage.

That'll please her, thought Eddie. The Hart men had an easy way when it came to disgruntling women.

His mind drifted back to his earlier meeting with Charlotte. She had agreed to a tour of the National Gallery, showing him some of her favourites. Their day started over drinks in Covent Garden. He told her about his week and the fire where they nearly lost one of the watch. She told him about a public enquiry her father had been asked to lead. He sat listening nervously, waiting for the inevitable question.

"So, what did you do yesterday?"

"I stayed home in the evening and, oh yes, lunchtime I went to see Nev. Remember, he had a stroke. They invited me."

Charlotte held her wine glass up to him. "Cheers," she said as their glasses clinked together. "Let's get going, there's much to see."

They glided through the rooms, stopping here for something diminutive, there for something grand. Eddie enjoyed the history and social context of the paintings more than a love for the art, which was obvious in Charlotte from her detailed descriptions and intense gaze. She was lost to them. For two hours, she exhausted him with her passion.

It wasn't until they stood in front of a self-portrait of Artemisia Gentileschi that she let her true feelings be known to him.

"I love this painting and I love this artist."

"Tell me about her."

"Artemisia Gentileschi, 1593–1653. She was taught by her artist father, who, by the time she was eighteen, declared her to be peerless amongst the artistic fraternity. At this time, she's raped in her studio by a man named Tassi. This rape was witnessed by others, so to save the Gentileschi name, he concedes to her father and agrees to marry her. Only when he reneges on the deal is he taken to court by the father."

"Wow."

"Wait, it gets better. During the court case, she is tortured. Tortured in front of the whole court to prove the veracity of her evidence. Not Tassi, not the witnesses, only her, the victim of the rape."

"How was she tortured?"

"Her arms tied to a chair and her fingers were slowly crushed, causing excruciating pain while being questioned."

"I take it she maintained her accusation."

"Of course, she did. So strong, yet so vulnerable."

"Vulnerable?"

"Yes, Eddie, vulnerable. Like all women then and since, vulnerable to the ideals, desires, and control of men. Their every whim."

"You're not, Charlotte."

"Oh really, Eddie, why not? I had a husband whose ideal marriage consisted of children, not just me, so on a whim, he changed me for another. You, Eddie, did I seem ideal at first, and have you come here today on a whim or a desire perhaps? The desire to bed me."

Eddie looked around him, embarrassed by the conversation.

"Let's sit down."

He gestured to the seating in the middle of the room.

"Why are you angry?"

"Tell me this, Eddie, and without thumbscrews, tell me the truth. If I hadn't asked you about yesterday, would you have told me, or would your lunch date with Jane have gone unmentioned?"

"It was with Nev, her husband, as well."

"Tell me."

Eddie looked back at Artemisia, staring at him across the centuries. If she had given in to the pain, said what the men wanted to hear, then her very soul would have been diminished.

"You're right, I'd have let it slide."

"I've been a fool."

"No, you haven't."

A panic rose quickly in his chest.

"What you've witnessed today is the worst of me, and I'm sorry for my foolishness. Please don't end this, let me prove to you how much I want this relationship."

"Do I look like her?"

"No, no."

"What is it then?"

"We were childhood sweethearts, and I have always looked back on that time."

"Why?"

He gazed into his lap. Charlotte could see his knuckles whiten as he gripped the edge of the leather seat.

"Because I was happy."

"Do you mean to tell me that since your childhood, no one has made you happy?"

"Yes, but not consistently. I have always been quick to fall in love and quick to fall out, but I hope you can forgive my mistake because I believe you are so very different. You can be my constant."

It was her turn to look back towards the painting. She seemed in communion with her heroine. Placing a hand on his, Charlotte spoke softly.

"Mio carissimo core."

Eddie didn't understand what she said, but it sounded positive.

"There ya go." Ray placed two steaming plates of food on the table. The beer had wet Eddie's appetite and he tucked into the food with gusto, which pleased his father.

"How was your day with Charlotte?"

"So so."

Ray stopped eating. "Don't tell me another one bites the dust."

"No, Dad, let's say our first argument. It ended on a positive note."

"Do you know I've never seen one of your girlfriends?"

"Well, let's change that, shall we?"

"Yea, it's time you stopped looking back, Son. Stop looking over your shoulder at your mother and me. Move on, Son."

"Yea, you're right, Dad, and I'm going to do my best. It's just hard, that's all."

"From contraction to committal, it's hard, Son."

"Alright, Sigmund Freud, what's the answer?"

"It's about acceptance. Accept the past, accept who you are and try to live a good life, which by the way, you do. Another sausage?"

Linsey sat in the car park outside the supermarket. She watched shoppers cram huge amounts of groceries into their cars. The prospect of running out of food when the shops closed for two days at Christmas couldn't be countenanced. In the vehicle next to her, a child sat in the elevated seat with a pack of twelve loo rolls squashed between its knees and the driver's seat. She smiled; the child stared back unmoved by her friendly gesture. Dad got in the driver's seat, and his door hit the side of Linsey's car. Normally, she wouldn't let that pass, but she couldn't have a contretemps with this stranger and risk missing Pat. There she was walking out the main doors with two large bags. Linsey jumped out of her car, her door hitting her opponent's. He wound down his window. "Oi, love!"

She leant in his window. "One each, call it a draw, shall we? I've got your number plate."

She hadn't, but it might stop an attempt to go two one up. "Pat." She caught up with Pat and walked alongside her. "Pat, can I have a word, please?" Pat kept walking.

"Two minutes, please, then I'll go."

Pat held out one of the bags. "Ain't got two minutes, so walk and talk." Linsey took the heavy bag.

"I just want to tell you that it all came to a head at work with Sean and he's gonna get what's coming to him. I want to say sorry again."

"That's where you're wrong, they never get what's coming."

"Well, he is in big trouble at work and I wanted you to know."

"Whatever it is, it's nothing to the trouble he causes outside work." Pat stopped and looked at Linsey. A pretty young thing with her life ahead of her. She envied her. Envied the choices she could still make. They stopped in front of Pat's house. She took back the bag of food.

"You got a fella?"

"No."

"Well, choose wisely. I don't know how, but make sure you do. Thanks for telling me and, well, just thanks." Pat smiled.

"Merry Christmas."

"Merry Christmas, Pat."

Pat turned and walked down her path. The door was opened by Ben. He looked at Linsey without any sign of emotion or recognition. Did she see in the briefest moment the eyes of his father? The door closed on their world as she turned to walk back to her car.

45

Harry was acting up one rank to a leading firefighter. Sean was off sick, and Chris had been suspended, pending an investigation. This meant all the Christmas leave was cancelled and a firefighter was needed to act as the leading firefighter, so all three appliances could be kept on the run. Harry was sitting in the watch room. He had attempted to sign off the petty cash. At the first attempt, it was two p out; the second try was twenty-one p out, so he decided to leave it for another officer.

"Ah, there you are, aitch. My car is still playing up. Any chance of a lift home tonight?"

Harry made out that the paperwork he was doing had been concluded satisfactorily. He placed his pen in the breast pocket of his shirt and spun his chair around from the desk.

"Well, Firefighter Dunstford, I'm not sure it's appropriate for an officer to mix with the rank and file."

Luke laughed. "You're such a bellend."

Eddie walked into the room, grabbed the tannoy mic, and asked for Linsey to go to the ADO's office.

"Did you hear that, Sub Officer? I do believe that is insubordination. Do you agree with me that he should be disciplined?"

"Possibly, Leading Firefighter, give me your detailed report in triplicate and I'll consider it."

Luke stood behind Eddie, giving Harry the wanker sign.

Linsey was sitting in the TV room with the rest of the watch when her name was called. She got up immediately. Perry, who was relaxing in a chair behind her, put out his hand as she passed him.

"Do you want me to come with you?"

"Nah, thanks, mate. I'm not the one who clocked him."

"No, but you were in the queue."

She smiled and left the room.

Clarence Siddall sat behind his desk. Arthur Church sat at the end of the desk. Both faced the door. Eddie Hart was on one side, next to the window. Outside, beneath the orange glow of the sodium street lamps, the commuters edged home for Christmas. Eddie's mobile rang.

"Sorry, Clarence, it's my dad. You ok, Dad?"

Ray was laughing. "A balti dish!"

"Well, you didn't want a coffee machine."

"Meena says it's rubbish."

"I still got the receipt, I'll change it for something else. I gotta go, Dad, busy."

"Ok, Son, you go, but I'm keeping it. See you soon."

The three officers knew it was overkill as they waited for Linsey. It was, however, a learning curve for them to be addressing a female firefighter, albeit all that was being requested was a written statement of the events in the leading firefighter's room and provide reassurance to her after the unpleasant incident.

Linsey knocked and walked into the room.

"Hallo, Linsey, please sit down. We won't keep you, but there are a few formalities regarding the incident with Sean and Chris," said Clarence. Linsey looked at Arthur and Eddie. Both smiled, she didn't.

"Firstly, are you ok? I know you didn't want to take the rest of the last tour off, but having spoken with HQ, everyone thought it appropriate."

Linsey nodded a yes and sat back against the chair while crossing her legs. "Good. Well, I'm afraid we will need a statement from you regarding the whole incident. Should you need any assistance compiling it in the rather formal way we use in the fire service, then please don't hesitate to ask any one of us here. Any questions?"

"Yes, when will Chris be back and why have I been told not to contact him?" The force of her question took Clarence by surprise. Arthur spoke.

"He'll be suspended until the enquiry is complete, Linsey, and we can't stop you contacting him, it was, let's say, thought best."

"Who by?"

"HR, I believe."

Clarence nodded.

"What will happen to him?"

"I couldn't possibly say," said the ADO.

Eddie watched from the side. He couldn't say he knew Linsey as well as the rest of the watch, but right now, he knew what was coming. He had dealt with pissed off firefighters many times over the years. Linsey was the first female but a firefighter nevertheless.

Linsey uncrossed her legs, looked up to the ceiling, then straight at Clarence.

Here we go, thought Eddie.

"Can we cut the crap?"

"I beg your pardon, Linsey," said Clarence.

"Oh, come on, Guvner, you know, you all know exactly what will happen. I bet it's already been decided and my report is a mere formality. I want to know what's happening with that creep Sean Stolly and I want to know if Chris' complaints will be taken seriously and dealt with, so he can get back to work soon."

"Firefighter Rivers, I…"

"Wait." Arthur, seeing how quickly it was deteriorating, stepped in. He knew Linsey deserved better.

"Linsey, I want to apologise to you. I have felt for a while that something was awry, and if I had addressed the coming storm, all this could have been averted. At one point, I thought the problem was between you and Chris. I know now how stupid that is, and again, I'm sorry. By the time I started asking questions about Sean, it was too late. You want it straight, Linsey, ok? After the week you've had, you deserve it. Sean has been transferred to a day work position at the BA training school. It hasn't been decided yet with Chris, but I'm confident in saying, best case scenario, he will be moved on to another watch; worst case, he will be demoted to firefighter and moved."

"Jesus wept, that vile man who subjected me to sexist, misogynistic behaviour, who subjected that lovely man Chris to sexist, homophobic behaviour, gets a nice job teaching BA. I hope the irony is not lost regarding that move. Meanwhile, Chris loses his job. Oh, and if I'm not mistaken, a job teaching BA comes with a promotion to Sub. Fuck sake, you couldn't make it up."

"Sean was hospitalised with a broken nose," said Clarence feebly.

"Good, it's the least he deserved."

"Why didn't you report anything, Linsey, earlier, and we've had no complaints from Chris?"

"With all due respect, Arthur, and I'm not blaming you in any way, but…" She stopped to compose herself. She looked at Eddie.

"Eddie, if you had beef with someone, would you go running to Arthur and you, Arthur, if you did, would you run to Clarence?"

Linsey looked at Clarence and wasn't so sure, but he, like the other two, held her gaze.

"Well, I'll tell ya. No, you wouldn't. We fight our corners, don't we? Plus, I'm a recruit, I'm new on the watch, and, surprise surprise, a woman. I want to fit in. I want to get on, be liked, not cause waves. How would it seem if I'd been here five minutes and I'm making complaints? I can just imagine, fuckin women, right?"

"We can't deal with it unless you tell us," said Clarence.

"You've got eyes, you've got ears, what you ain't got is the guts to call out a problem like Stolly, and I'm talking about the service. He's a problem that's just moved on every time the shit hits. He's getting away with it, don't you see that, and good people are left damaged because of it." Linsey stood up as she reached the peak of her anger.

"I came into this job and thought I'd found my purpose in life, a noble profession, and it is. What I didn't realise is, it's run like some private gentleman's club where it's not what you know but who you know. Well, that ain't for me, I'd rather drive a bus. My notice will be on your desk at the end of this tour, Sir. Arthur, Eddie." Linsey turned and walked out.

The three men looked at one another.

"That went well," said Eddie.

"Bloody hell, are we that bad?" Clarence threw his pen onto the desk.

"I'd say that is blatantly obvious," said Arthur.

"I missed so much, so wrapped up in myself, Christ sake," said Eddie.

He got up to follow her. "Fuck that, we ain't losing her."

"Eddie." Arthur stayed his sub officer by grabbing his arm. "Let her cool down, then we will both have a word, cos you're right, we ain't losing that one."

Linsey walked out into the yard. The early evening air was like a splash of cold water on her face. Luke had his bonnet up, tinkering.

"Alright, Lazy?"

"Alright, Puke."

"Got plans over the festive season?"

"Not a great deal. I will spend tomorrow night at my parents with my brothers and their families. Dad loves it when we are all together, and he can prepare a huge turkey. He loves watching us all sitting at his table, chatting away."

"What do you chat about, Lins?"

"Oh, you know the usual, kids, work, the future."

He noticed her looking at the stars in the clear night sky.

"Making a wish for Christmas?"

"Yea, I guess so."

"What ya wishing for? Come on, you can tell me."

"Oh, let's think; peace on earth and goodwill to all men."

"Fuck me, that's the sort of thing my misses says. How you supposed to wrap that up? Women!"

The bells went down and Harry announced over the tannoy, "All three flat fire in the high-rise at Courtlands."

The bay doors opened, and the three fire engines of Red Watch Langden pulled out of the fire station and slipped into the traffic. Arthur hit the two tones, and the crocodile of commuter vehicles in the night's heavy commute moved to the kerb and central reservation to let them through, assisting with the need to help someone in trouble.

ADO Clarence Siddall, now alone in the station, went to the watch room and looked at the printout of the fire call. He considered going too, then decided he would wait for Arthur's first message before making that decision. He walked out into the bay, closing each door in turn. With the station secure, he went back to his office and the endless paperwork.

THE END